Who Are You?
and Why Should I Care?

Learning to Lead as You Have Never Led Before

By Dr. Clinton M. Covert

Dedication

To Marian

ISBN : 978-1-967778-09-6

The life which is unexamined is not worth living."

\- **Socrates**

PREFACE

A single definition of leadership remains elusive. Different theories and models of leadership abound. Some are prescriptive. They attempt to tell people *how* to lead. While some outline *where* or *when* to employ a particular leadership style, others list *what* traits or characteristics make up great leaders. Finally, multiple models and different theories include literature that expounds on the *why* of leadership. The author in this book argues that all these models and methods have their place because leadership is multi-faceted. However, what is missing is an examination of the *who* of leadership.

Who am I? Many live out their lives without ever taking the time to self-reflect and pose this question to themselves. Not knowing the answer to this question is unfortunate. Seeking answers to who we are helps us better understand who we have been, who we are now, and who we aspire to be. We cannot reach our full potential without a deep understanding of this. Knowing who we are grounds our actions and provides a roadmap for pursuing what inspires us. We will be unable to realize our purpose without such an understanding. We will also be unable to lead effectively and encourage others.

At its foundation, leadership is about getting someone to do something. While leadership involves inspiring others, it is also about leading yourself. To motivate others, we must first understand what drives us. Therefore, this book focuses on the *who* part of leadership. Instead of telling you how to lead or listing the type of personality traits that will best serve you with different people, places, or situations, my aim in the pages that follow is to demonstrate that, at its core, leadership is about first understanding who you are. Yes, leadership is complex. It is also hard to master. However, this endeavor to understand oneself lies at the heart of the human condition and, when done well, leads to personal growth and fulfillment.

Leadership comes in many forms and is an ongoing pursuit – it never stops. When leaders become complacent, they run the risk of failure. With leadership, there are no do-overs, only chances to self-correct and do better next time. Because none of us are perfect and without flaws, knowing who you are involves acknowledging your imperfections while capitalizing on your strengths. Operating from within your true self is the first step in getting others to care enough about you to follow you as their leader; hence, the title of this book.

Because most life challenges are unplanned, we must confront issues as they occur. Life's unpredictability could mean that something is coming your way right now! This "something" will significantly impact your professional and personal life, whether a personal crisis or leadership challenge. It may even occur while reading this book! And you have to be prepared for such a crisis. Knowing who you are will allow you to overcome whatever challenges you inevitably face. If you agree that this is worth investing your time in, I encourage you to turn the page and read the remainder of this book. Doing so will teach you to lead as you have never led before.

Richmond, Virginia

"If your actions inspire others to dream more, learn more, do more, and become more, you are a leader."

– John Quincy Adams

ABOUT THE AUTHOR

Dr. Clinton M. Covert is originally from Corning, New York, and has held multiple federal government positions in equal employment opportunity and leadership development across the Department of Defense (DoD) during a twenty-year career. In this capacity, he oversaw developing and enforcing policies and programs that make it illegal to discriminate against current employees and applicants for employment as mandated by federal laws, rules, and regulations.

Dr. Covert is also a twenty-year Army veteran and has served in diverse leadership positions and organizations. Before retiring from the Army in 2003, he was featured in SOLDIER Magazine for his educational accomplishments as an enlisted soldier while serving on active duty. In addition to holding a doctorate in Education from the University of Southern California and a master's in Human Relations from the University of Oklahoma, he has completed numerous federal government leadership development programs. These include the Army Command and General Staff College's Leadership, Education, and Development (LEAD) course, the Organizational Leadership for Executives (OLE) program, and the Sustaining Base Leadership and Management (SBLM) course.

Dr. Covert is a Department of Defense Executive Leadership Development Program (DLDP) graduate and a non-residence Air

Command and Staff College (ACSC) graduate. In 2008, the United States Equal Employment Opportunity Commission (EEOC) selected him to serve as its Meritorious Research Fellow. He has also recently completed his Society of Human Resource Management-Certified Professional (SHRM-CP) and Certified Diversity Professional (CDP) certifications.

In his spare time, he enjoys drawing and reading about all things related to the history of Porsche automobiles. However, in 2014, at 49, he found a new hobby – running. Within five years, he completed one full marathon and twenty half marathons across the United States. Dr. Covert and his wife Marian have been married for over 35 years and reside near Richmond, Virginia.

In May 2017, Dr. Covert attended Harvard University's Senior Executive Fellows (SEF). In 2021, his military and civilian careers culminated with him achieving his longtime goal of being able to attend and graduate from the National War College at Fort McNair in Washington, D.C., something he was ineligible to participate in as an enlisted Soldier during his time in the Army. During these courses, graduates were encouraged to identify their passions and purpose. The programs served as accelerators for him to write this book.

"Leadership is not about titles, positions or flowcharts. It is about one life influencing another."

– John C. Maxwell

ACKNOWLEDGMENTS

Writing a book is similar to running a marathon. First, you have to want to do it. Second, you need to have a plan. Third, you have to apply what you have learned along the way as part of your growth in overcoming obstacles. The ability to persist is always more a mental achievement than a physical one. However, the essential thing for publishing a book or crossing the finish line in a marathon is taking the first step.

To a large extent, writing a book or running a marathon are individual endeavors; you either complete these challenges or do not. Close associates have asked me what I think about while I am running. My reply is always the same: "Putting one foot in front of the other." Metaphorically, writing a book is like taking one step at a time.

However, aspiring authors and runners will be unable to realize their goals without the help of others. Writers require trusted advisors' critical eyes and feedback along the way, much like the water stations and cheering sections at a marathon. To all of those who have taken the time to read earlier drafts, I want to express my sincere appreciation for helping me cross the finish line. You know who you are.

Table of Contents

INTRODUCTION

Everyone has a story to tell. And yet, countless stories go untold. It is unfortunate, given the missed opportunities for learning and growth for the storyteller and everyone at the receiving end of the story. In a way, storytelling is part of leadership. Our stories tell others who we are. They can inspire and push us forward in life's journeys and pursuits. Life stories also provide fresh perspectives on a leadership challenge or problem.

The trials and tribulations of others can serve as affirmations for our life path or as a stimulus to make course corrections. Narrating these stories gives us authenticity in leading others. Intuitively, it offers others pause when deciding whether to follow someone as their leader. Knowing who we are informs our stories. Before telling our stories, we must ask ourselves, "Who am I?" Our stories can resonate with others when we have grasped this deep understanding of ourselves.

Since this is a book about leadership, it will focus on exploring the *who* aspect of leadership. While the other aspects of leadership – the what, how, and why – are all interconnected, I believe the *who* part determines how we respond within a leadership framework encompassing all these elements.

Again, the best leaders tell stories - they do so to create deeper connections by being more relatable to their audience on a human level. By telling others about ourselves, we become more credible; we inspire trust. Relatable experiences give the leader's story meaning and make the message more impactful.

Accordingly, this book contains portions of my life story. First, I use a combination of fictional and non-fictional accounts, vignettes, and other illustrations as a segue to introduce the specific concepts about leadership covered in each chapter. Second, I use it to illustrate the role of the *who* aspect of leadership to establish trustworthiness with you, the reader. The non-fictional stories herein are real. While portions protect the identities of individuals, the descriptions of these people and events remain intact. The reality within the vignettes and fictional accounts also remains.

At this point, some of you are probably saying to yourselves, "We are who we are!" Implicit in this declaration is the foregone conclusion that individuals cannot change. With this belief, it would be easy to question the utility of reading any further. Yes, we are who we are. However, this statement alone does not go far enough in answering the question, "Who are you?"

Who we are does not remain static. Our good and bad choices, successes and failures, and other lived experiences make us who we are today as we become who we are supposed to be. If actions cause reactions and choices to have consequences, understanding who you are will form a connection to all the other elements that make up effective leadership.

I recently participated in a job interview for a promotion. The leader of the three-member hiring panel started with, "Tell us about yourself." In essence, they were asking, "Who are you?" My response to this question also answered this book's subtitle, "Why should I care?" What about me moves them to select me for the position over the other applicants?

The interview continued with the hiring officials posing situational leadership questions. It concluded with one of the members asking, "Tell me about a time when you faced an ethical dilemma; what did you do, and what was the outcome?" Again, my answer revealed who I was as an individual and a leader. Such questions evoke responses that show others what you value. They also provide a snapshot of how your moral compass guides your actions in confronting and overcoming ethical dilemmas and other life challenges. My responses also told them *why* I was the best selection for the position.

While writing this book, I engaged in multiple conversations with myself and thought a lot about leadership. I also reflected on what makes good and bad leaders. All the while, I mentally balanced the type of leader I am with the one I aspire to be. In getting to the core of what makes some individuals better leaders than others, I shifted my focus from external factors, such as work environments or other individuals, to an internal examination of myself. Along the way, it struck me how so many variables and forces lie beyond my control. My self-reflection reinforced something I intuitively already knew. As a leader of myself and others, the only thing I can control is me.

This shift in perspective led me to focus more and more on answering the question, "Who am I?"

Getting the most out of this book will require you to self-reflect throughout each chapter. You will also need to be truly honest with yourself. Candidness with yourself will not always be easy. You will have to revisit things from your past that you had forgotten about or wish to keep suppressed. As William Nerin notes in *You Can't Grow Up Till You Go Back Home*, who we are encompasses two parts. One part is our mother and father. Environmental factors influence the second part. Together, the parts form our unique selves. Both parts shape our sense of who we are and our self-esteem. While reading this book, resurfacing the feelings attached to your fears, past slights, failures, and regrets is the first step in overcoming the impediments to having higher self-esteem, personal growth, and becoming a better leader. The good news is that you only have to be honest with yourself!

A process model for learning comprises three components: readiness, experience, and reflection. According to this model, this middle "experience" stage or learning activity is you reading this book. This stage also includes completing the exercises at the end of each chapter with sincere and honest self-reflection.

The first component of the model, the "readiness" stage, requires the learner (you, the reader) to answer the following:

(1) How *ready* are you?

(2) *How* are you ready?

(3) How *open* are you?

(4) How *present* are you?

(5) What are your *expectations*?

(6) *Why* are you reading this book?

(7) *How* are you reading this book?

The final component, or the "reflection" stage, requires you to apply your learning. Answering the following questions will guide the learning outcomes for this stage.

(1) *Will* you do anything with what you have learned?

(2) *What* will you do with what you have learned?

(3) *How* will you make sense of what you have learned?

(4) *With whom* will you apply what you have learned?

(5) What will you *do* differently?

(6) How will you *be* different?

(7) How will you *lead* differently?

Accordingly, at the end of each chapter, I will offer practical exercises to assist you in gaining a deeper appreciation for understanding *who* you are. An essential part of this book will be the time spent reflecting on what you just read and responding to the questions at the end. These questions will serve as a starting point to further explore your emotions that surface during quiet reflection. While determining the root cause of these feelings, you will identify what you have learned from these experiences and understand what you can do differently moving forward.

Finally, one risk of writing a book is that it can quickly become an exercise in vanity. To guard against this, I intentionally try to write for my audience, you, the reader. You will be the judge if I succeed in doing so. Let's begin!

<u>**EXERCISE**</u>

Self-reflection entails asking yourself questions about your values, assessing your strengths and failures, and thinking about your perceptions and interactions with others. Take a moment to read, think about, and answer the below questions. Again, there are no CORRECT answers; there are only YOUR answers. Record your responses in as much detail as possible while being honest with yourself.

Over time, what factors or events have shaped your understanding of who you are?

____

____

____

____

____

If someone were to ask you, who are you? What would you say? Why?

____

____

____

____

____

What people or events have propelled you in your leadership journey from early childhood to now? Who? How?

____

____

____

____

____

What people or events beginning in early childhood have inhibited or impeded your ability to grow personally and professionally? Who? How?

____

____

____

____

____

If I were to ask one of your subordinates, colleagues, bosses, and close family members to define who you are, what would each of them say? Why?

____

____

____

____

____

Would what others say about you align with what you say about yourself? How? If not, why?

____

____

____

____

What are your values? What is important to you? Why?

____

____

____

Do your values align with who you say you are? How? If not, why?

Now, take a moment to reflect on what you have written and answer the following questions:

What parts of your responses surprised you? Why?

What parts of your responses would you like to change? Why?

____

____

____

____

____

Record your thoughts and feelings after having taken part in this exercise. How did answering the questions and reflecting on your answers make you feel? Why?

____

____

____

____

____

PART ONE

Who Are You?

"It's not about the cards you're dealt, but how you play the hand."

– Randy Pausch, The Last Lecture

CHAPTER 1

Do you Know Who I Am?

The University of Southern California professor stood before his class on a Monday morning and announced to the 100 students present, "This Friday will be your final exam. This exam will begin precisely at nine o'clock and will end at eleven o'clock sharp. By the way, this exam will count toward 50 percent of your final grade. So, Trojans, see you on Friday!" Shortly after, the 100 students filed out of the stadium-seating auditorium. Friday came, and 99 of the 100 students arrived a few minutes before nine. They proceeded down the aisles to the front, where the professor stood behind the podium. They each stopped at the table nearby, picked up a copy of the exam, returned up the aisles to their assigned seats, and started taking the exam.

Around ten o'clock, the remaining student casually strolled into the classroom. Without urgency, he walked to the front of the auditorium, picked up a test, and returned to his seat. Student 100 did not feel compelled to offer any apology or explanation to the professor about why he was late.

At eleven o'clock, the professor instructed, "Stop! Put your pens and papers down. Proceed to the front and turn in your exam." The first 99 students did exactly that. As these students exited the auditorium, the professor stood down front, arranging the papers in an orderly stack. He stopped abruptly when, out of the corner of his eye, he saw Student 100 still sitting in his seat, taking the exam. The professor shouted, "Young man, didn't I tell you you would have your final exam on Friday? Didn't I also tell you that this exam would start precisely at nine o'clock and end exactly at eleven? Not only have you failed to follow the instructions, but you have also failed this course. I'll see you again next term!"

Student 100 exited his seat, walked down the aisle, and stopped before the professor. With his chest out, he pointed at the professor and asked in a raised voice, "Do you know who I am?!" The student's demeanor and questions took the professor by surprise. After a slight pause to get his bearings, the professor's voice got louder with each word as he responded, "I most certainly do not. And to tell you the truth, young man, I REALLY DON'T CARE!"

With a smirk, the student went to where the professor stood with his neatly stacked papers. He lifted part of the stack, inserted his test in the middle, and dropped the remaining tests on the pile. Then, knowing the professor did not know his name, the student said, "That's exactly what I thought!" With that, he exited the auditorium.

When I conduct training, I tell this story to leaders as a cautionary tale of what can happen when we do not know those we lead. In this scenario, the professor had not taken the time to learn the names of all his students, let alone anything personal about them. Predictably, the answer to the student's question to the professor, "Do you know who I am?" drove what happened next. The professor not knowing anything about the student – not even his name – led to a poor outcome regarding both the student's class experience and the professor's ability to hold the student accountable for his actions.

As a leader, an equally important question is, "Who are you?" Answering this question requires a candid assessment of yourself. Some of the answers may lead to feeling a certain level of discomfort as we face our shortcomings. However, the willingness to recognize our flaws offers opportunities for change. Understanding who we are develops our authentic selves as leaders and why those we lead should care. To this topic, I now turn.

"Get comfortable being uncomfortable."

– Navy SEAL

Getting Comfortable

I once trained with the Navy SEALs. I was competitively selected to participate in the Department of Defense (DoD) Executive Leadership Development Program (ELDP) earlier that year. This ten-month program exposes future senior civilian leaders to the challenges our military's warfighters face. For two weeks each month, 50 mid-level federal government employees from 26 federal agencies across the Department went to locations across the United States and overseas where service members worked.

At our orientation meeting in Washington, D.C., that year, the program's director congratulated us on our selection. Then, after going over the program's upcoming schedule and other administrative details, she concluded by remarking, "All of you have just won the lottery!" I was unsure of what she meant by this at the time, but during the next ten months, I would understand why she had made this proclamation.

As a Secretary of Defense program under the Office of the Undersecretary of Defense for Personnel and Readiness, ELDP trains through immersion. It was an opportunity for us to see the Department through the eyes of Soldiers, Marines, Sailors, Airmen, and members of the Coast Guard. The program centered on us students learning through up-close and hands-on experiences. The primary objective of ELDP was to expose emerging senior leaders to the challenges service members face and how other branches of the government operate to support the military. This exposure allows the ELDP graduate to fulfill future roles as senior civilian leaders helping those on the front lines defending our nation.

We visited Lexington and Concord, where we learned about the birth of our nation and the sacrifices our forefathers made for freedom. While at the Demilitarized Zone in the Republic of Korea, we visited the United Nations building at the Joint Security Area at Panmunjom. While inside, the only thing that separated us from the North Korean guards was the windows of the building. After visiting Pearl Harbor on Pearl Harbor Day, we honored the fallen sailors who sank at the USS Arizona Memorial. We toured the United States Naval Academy in Annapolis to observe how one military service educates young men and women to become future military leaders.

We had an early morning rude awakening by the marine drill instructors at Camp Pendleton, California.

With the guidance of the Army Ranger Training Brigade, each team conquered the Malvesti Obstacle Course and then rappelled down the 30-foot and 70-foot Ranger training towers at Fort Benning, Georgia. Army Rangers are part of the United States Army Special Operations Command (USASOC), with the Army's Ranger course preparing officers and enlisted Soldiers to conduct missions involving unconventional warfare, counterinsurgency, foreign internal defense, and other specialized tasks.

At Vandenburg Air Force Base, California, we toured the launch site where a Delta II rocket was preparing for a mission and learned about the Air Force's space and missile heritage. In Arizona, we had the privilege of training with the U.S. Border Patrol. Next, we visited Brussels, Belgium, the capital of the European Union. Then, on a staff ride to Butte de Lion, more commonly known as the Battle of Waterloo, we learned about Napoleon Bonaparte's defeat by the combined armies of the Seventh Coalition. We received briefings on the importance of international partnerships at the North Atlantic Treaty Organization (NATO) Headquarters and the Supreme Headquarters Allied Powers Europe (SHAPE). Then, after learning how the military plans for future wars at the Pentagon in Washington, D.C., we participated in a staff ride to Gettysburg. At our commencement ceremony in Washington, D.C., in June 2011, the ELDP Director's words came back into my mind. Yes, it indeed felt like we had won the lottery!

While in Coronado, a SEAL cadre member directed our cohort to change into military combat uniforms. Navy SEALs, which stands for Sea, Land, and Air, are the United States Navy's primary special operations force and a component of the United States Navy Special Warfare Command. After leading us in various exercises, the SEAL took us outside the compound, where we ran up and down the beach in a military formation. After running for about two miles, we stopped and stood before three large poles lying on the sand. My cohort then dispersed around the poles in groups of seven or eight on each side facing the ocean. Then, the cadre told us to lift the 480-pound pole and stand directly underneath it with our arms extended above our heads. The Navy SEAL instructed us to lower the pole to our right shoulder through a bullhorn microphone when he commanded, "Down!" We pressed the pole above our heads when he next commanded, "Up!" We lowered the pole to our left shoulder on the following "Down!" command. The raising and lowering of the pole went on for what seemed like a very long time.

As each team increasingly struggled as time passed, a thought raced through my mind. I remember asking myself, how could I be so *uncomfortable* in a place where most people come to be relaxed and *comfortable*? I was on the beautiful Coronado Pacific Beach near San Diego, yet I was soaked in sweat, my heart racing, and my muscles aching. My thoughts quickly faded from my mind as the instructor ordered us to put the poles down and proceed to the obstacle course.

Later that afternoon, we broke into teams of seven personnel, with one Navy SEAL assigned to each group for water raft relays. The relays involved lifting the rafts above our heads, carrying the float to the ocean, paddling to a turnaround point, and returning to shore. We quickly learned that the key to not having your small boat capsize was ensuring that the front of the float directly faced the incoming 8–10 feet-high surface waves. Every crew member's paddle had to be synchronized, and we had to work as a team. Any deviation from this would indeed overturn the raft.

As we finished this task, I saw the SEAL candidate assigned to my float team gazing out into the distance. He was looking at a group of SEAL candidates on the beach rolling around in the sand. They waded into the ocean for hours, rolled around in the sand, and did pushups and other exercises. They were wet, cold, and looked miserable. The SEAL candidate assigned to our group was on medical holdover for an injury. He would have to remain in this status for a couple of months until the next cycle of recruits. He could have withdrawn from the course; he chose to stay.

When we prepared to depart later that day, the SEAL candidates were still going at it on the beach. One of the SEAL cadre members explained the reason behind this drill to us. The candidates confronting and overcoming such a demanding and rigorous assessment would train them to *become comfortable with being uncomfortable*. Over time, this saying has become a leadership rallying cry across sectors and settings by individuals and groups. The statement now risks becoming trite and losing its impact. However, as I have thought about the different aspects of leadership, this concept still resonates with me and plays a significant role in the focus of this book – the *who* part of leadership.

Exploring who we are necessitates discomfort, and the willingness to sit in the discomfort of uncertainty requires courage. To seek the answers to who we are propels us to revisit some things we would rather leave in the past. But this is the first step. By becoming comfortable with being uncomfortable, we can identify our true selves. By looking inward, we come to have a better understanding of who we are. Remembering the life experiences that have had the most impact on shaping who we are today leads us toward developing our authentic selves.

Self-authenticity is something I will explore further in Chapter 2. This exploration of coming to know who you are as a person brings clarity and purpose to who you are as a leader. Most of us have the desire to learn new things. What we often overlook is learning more about ourselves. Knowing our strengths, weaknesses, and fears allows us to cope better with life's challenges and how we relate to others. In doing so, we improve our relationship with those we lead. More importantly, we develop our relationship with ourselves.

Early in my career, one of my biggest fears was rejection – not getting selected for a professional development opportunity, a job promotion, or not receiving praise or recognition from my parents or others whose opinions I valued. To this day, rejection still stings. However, I understand the feelings associated with fear are not unique to me. All of us fear something. The question is, how do we harness our fear in order not to become immobilized?

I do not allow this feeling to paralyze me from pursuing my dreams and goals. For example, I was unsuccessful when I first applied for the above "lottery" course. A year after not being selected,

I changed the date on my application and resubmitted it. Nothing in my application package had changed, but the second time I applied, I was selected and participated in the program. Today, I tell this story to those I lead. I do so to inspire them to push through when confronting rejection in their own personal and professional lives.

The second fear of mine is the fear of failure – failing to succeed in a new job or failing to lead others to reach their full potential. As I write these pages, I am fearful, questioning myself, and unsure if anyone will read this book. And if they do, I fear they will be uninspired to continue reading. Self-doubt washes over me as I wonder if they will get anything out of it. To manage my fears, I must first identify and acknowledge them. Only then can I develop strategies to overcome them. For me, I have come to believe that to reach my full potential, I must have faith. I must put myself in the game. I now realize there will be setbacks, but rejection and failure are part of the leadership journey.

When I experience these feelings today, I ask myself, "What is the worst that can happen?" The answers provide me with a level of comfort while being uncomfortable. I will apply again if I am not accepted for a school or job promotion. If I fail at something, I will learn from my mistakes and use what I have learned moving forward. And if no one reads this book, it will not have been a wasted endeavor, for I will have learned more about myself. When it comes to fear, I find it helpful to remind myself of what Ralph Waldo Emerson said, "It was high counsel that I once heard given to a young person, `always do what you are afraid to do.'"

Obstacles are part of our personal growth. Because all of us are unique individuals, different things make each of us uncomfortable. What is essential is first identifying what these things are to reflect on how to become comfortable with being uncomfortable. As Susan Peppercorn notes in her paper, *How to Overcome Your Fear of Failure*, "…it's when you feel comfortable that you should be fearful because it's a sign that you're not stepping far enough out of your comfort zone to take steps that will help you rise and thrive."

This chapter lays the foundation for what follows in the remaining parts of this book. While Chapter 1 sets the stage for answering the question in the title of this book, Chapter 2 provides an opportunity to explore further what we do and do not know about ourselves. We must understand ourselves before asking others the question in this book's title. In the following pages, we will explore the concepts of "blind spots" and the Johari window framework to bring clarity and purpose to *who* we are as a leader. But first, take a moment to answer the questions in the exercise given below.

<u>EXERCISE</u>

From a leadership perspective, please write down 10 to 20 short statements on what you believe about leadership based on who you are.

1. I believe

____

2. I believe

____

3. I believe

____

4. I believe

____

5. I believe

____

6. I believe

____

7. I believe

____

8. I believe

____

9. I believe

____

10. I believe

____

11. I believe

____

12. I believe

____

13. I believe

____

14. I believe

____

15. I believe

____

16. I believe

____

17. I believe

____

18. I believe

____

19. I believe

____

20. I believe

____

Do these statements have elements of what you listed earlier as your values? How? If not, why?

____

____

____

____

What makes you uncomfortable in your personal and professional life? Why?

____

____

____

____

What was your biggest leadership fear? How did you confront or overcome it? What did you learn?

____

____

____

What is your most significant leadership fear that you have yet to overcome? What do you fear will happen if you do it?

____

____

____

____

What would be the benefits of the effort to overcome this fear versus the cost of a missed opportunity? Elaborate.

____

____

____

____

What impact have these things had on your personal and professional growth?

____

____

____

____

What impact have these things had on your ability to lead others? How?

____

____

____

____

What strategies and specific actions will you implement to become comfortable being uncomfortable in your personal and professional life?

____

____

____

In my journal for the above exercise, I recorded the following about what I believe:

Everyone makes mistakes.

Everyone deserves a second chance.

There is good in everyone.

We are all flawed.

We are all a work in progress.

We can accomplish anything we put our minds to.

Life is short.

We are here to make a difference in others' lives.

Someone is always watching you.

Trust is paramount in any relationship.

It is tough to get back once trust is broken.

You have to stand for something.

The truth will set you free.

Life has highs and lows.

We should learn from our mistakes.

Without hope, there is only despair.

Fear is the most significant barrier to realizing our full potential.

Being a true leader is hard work.

Nothing stays the same.

We cannot reach our full potential without the help of others.

We should be nice to each other.

We do not know what we do not know.

We can remain stuck in the past.

Our lives have a purpose.

We should be passionate about something.

Take a moment to reflect on what you have written. These responses are your gut reaction to the question and are a good benchmark for your current leadership beliefs. They are primarily your orientation and guide how you interact with yourself and others daily.

CHAPTER 2

Blind Spots

Early in the Gulf War, I watched as the then Secretary of Defense, Donald Rumsfeld, held court within the Pentagon's briefing room. His daily pontifications to the assembled press members ranged from the bizarre to the profound. One day, he began rambling when answering a question from one of the reporters about how well the war campaign was going. As if he was working out his answer aloud, Rumsfeld said, "There are known knowns. These are things we know that we know. There are known unknowns. That is to say, there are things that we know we don't know. But there are also unknown unknowns. There are things we don't know, we don't know..."

I remember thinking his response was a bunch of mumble jumble designed to evade or deflect the question. Therefore, I categorized Rumsfeld's answer as being somewhat bizarre. However, his reply that day stuck with me over the years. Years later, I recall thinking more about these "unknowns" as part of my self-reflection about leadership. What I once viewed as an evasive answer, I now look at as having substance, especially about leaders' blind spots. Over time, I came to understand the importance of the concept of leaders not knowing what they do not know. This recognition is paramount as leaders operate within the "battlefield" of influencing others to achieve the desired goal or end state. Understanding what we do not know about ourselves is just as important as learning and knowing about external factors that impact our ability to lead.

These "blind spots" impede our ability to maximize our influence over ourselves and others. Therefore, we must be receptive to activities and processes that expose our "unknown" areas to overcome this. Identifying these gaps can take place through self-reflection and feedback from others. Over the years, I have modeled some of the tenets of this phenomenon in workshops and training classes.

In my current job, I conduct training about equal employment opportunity and diversity in the workplace. I begin every training session by asking the class to participate in an exercise involving questions about me. I do this as an "icebreaker" to initiate class participation and facilitate discussions that follow emotionally charged and controversial topics such as race and valuing diversity. I ask those in attendance to write down their initial or "gut" responses to seven questions.

First, I ask them what my race is. Then, I ask participants to write down my age. Next, I asked them what city or town I consider my home of record. Once they have recorded their answers on the paper in front of them, I ask the students to write down my number of marriages. I then ask how many kids I have. This line of questioning continues with me asking participants if they think I speak a second language. For those who believe I do, I ask them to write down what language it is. Finally, I concluded this exercise by asking those in attendance to identify my education level.

Once they have their responses, I ask them to share them aloud. I list their assumptions on a whiteboard as they shout them out to me and allow the class to review all the responses. Once considered, I lead the class to discuss the answers to these questions. No one ever comes close to getting all of them correct.

In the ten-plus years I have done this exercise, most individuals only get one or two questions correct. For example, responses to the question about my race include white or Caucasian, Spanish, Arabic, Hispanic, Greek, Italian, and Portuguese. Once I explained the differences between race and national origin categories, I told the class that my father was white and my mother's maiden name was Sepulveda. She is originally from Zwolle, Louisiana, and is part Spanish and part American Indian.

Responses to the question about my age range from 35 to 60 years old over the years facilitating this class. I am currently 59. Mostly, people assume I am from New York, Florida, Texas, or California. However, class participants often also list Greece and Spain as my home of origin. I tell the class that I was born in Montour Falls, New York, and grew up in Corning, New York.

On average, about one-third of respondents correctly answered that I have been married only once. Over two-thirds of each class assumes I have somewhere between two to four kids when my wife and I do not have any. Less than a third respond correctly by stating that I do not speak a second language, with the remainder proclaiming that I must speak Spanish or Arabic. Finally, less than one-third correctly responded that I hold a doctorate. However, the average response rate for this last question is somewhat skewed. Many in the group who answered this question correctly confessed that they saw me exiting my car in the parking lot before the start of class and noticed my "DR CLINT" Virginia state license plate. Yes, *someone is always watching you*!

Words matter. Context also matters. Knowing who you are will ensure your words, actions, and deeds align. Since this is a book about leadership, I will cover this concept in further detail in the following pages.

This initial exercise spurs a more open dialogue for the remainder of the class. Often, a robust discussion follows when I ask, "What is the purpose of this exercise?" First, we talk about the different dimensions of diversity. We then talk about how our life experiences to date shape our responses. The discussion then turns to how we all try to derive meaning from what we see before us. Next, we discuss what it means to make assumptions and explore the differences between prejudice and discrimination. Often, the discussion turns to how our attitudes toward these different dimensions of diversity can drive our behavior. Inevitably, someone will yell something like, "We don't know what we don't know!" That is the exercise's point. I challenge the participants to question their blind spots, deeply held assumptions, and fixed beliefs. It is what Tony Schwartz, in his article, *What It Takes to Think Deeply About Complex Problems*, refers to as *deepening* – developing our capacity to *see* more.

I conclude this classroom exercise by emphasizing the need to guard against making assumptions. Instead of relying on our "gut," I suggest a better way is to engage in a personal conversation with those around us. These conversations are crucial when we assign negative connotations to our assumptions based on stereotypes. As a leader, stereotyping or applying generalizations about how people of a given gender, race, religion, or national origin look, think, or act creates barriers to effectively leading individuals and teams. Like the students in this classroom experience, our assumptions are often incorrect. *We don't know what we don't know.*

What we think we know is informed by mental models shaped by our values, beliefs, identity, life history, and experiences beginning in early childhood. The latter tells how our narratives develop, and our role models direct our paths forward. Through this lens of judging and perceiving is how we view the world. Our worldview does not necessarily remain static; it can change as our lens widens through new experiences that impact how we perceive and judge our surroundings, as depicted in Figure 1.

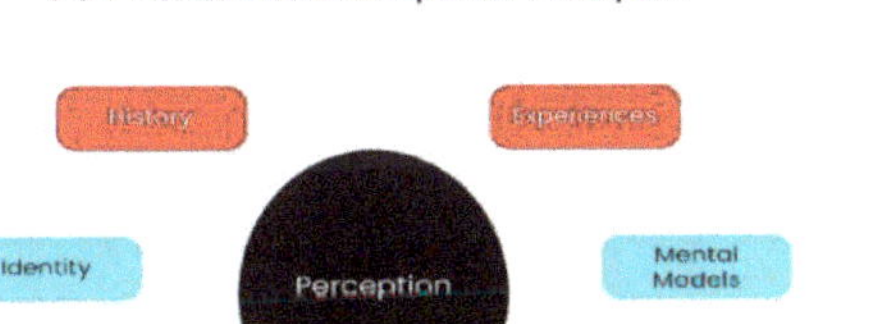

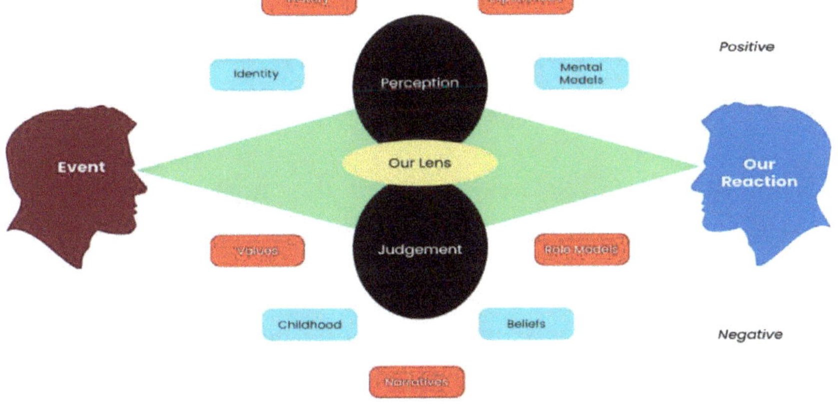

Figure 1

As leaders, we fail if we do not get to know those we lead. Everyone has a story. Within these stories are each of our fears, hopes, and dreams. Taking the time to understand what motivates those you lead is an investment with a huge return. The payout comes in getting them to commit fully to you as their leader. It is also an opportunity for you to guide their path in realizing their dreams. Knowing what makes people tick is more of an art than a science. At the same time, great leaders must never use this information for nefarious reasons. The most critical component is developing the discipline to listen deeply to those you lead.

Active Listening

As Bryant McGill states, "One of the most sincere forms of respect is actually listening to what another person has to say." Marshall Goldsmith, in *What Got You Here, Won't Get You There*, implores leaders to break from "bad habits" and learn to listen more. Active listening is the process of parroting back what the other person has expressed to let them know you are listening and to check your understanding of their meaning. More specifically, active listening involves restating the other person's communication while being aware of the accompanying feelings of nonverbal cues such as tone of voice, facial expressions, and body posture.

While working in the federal government, I worked in different types of agencies and military services with unique missions. Yet, no matter the size or geographical location, all these jobs had one thing in common – people. To be successful, leaders at every level must understand and know how to effectively communicate with individuals from diverse backgrounds while meeting individual's divergent needs and managing competing agendas. Successfully doing this is no small feat. Many folks value the "dynamic" leader who can articulate a strategic vision that compels others to work toward a stated goal. So, effective oral and written communication is a "must" for leaders to inspire others to act. But just as important is active listening.

I once received a job promotion at an agency that was different from my past assignments. The position required me to learn a new organizational mission, structure, and operating procedures. All the while, the expectation at this level was that you would come in and "hit the ground running." One week into my new job, my boss called me the morning of a meeting requiring his presence and instructed me to attend in his place. It was not uncommon for my boss, the Director of EEO, to have me, as his deputy, participate in meetings on his behalf. What was unusual was that he did not give me any forewarning or insight into what he knew would happen next.

The week prior, my boss and the Director of Human Capital had gotten into a spat at one of the senior leader meetings. The agency head directed them to devise a fix to the problem and report back to her at the next meeting. Unfortunately, the two directors had not "ironed it out" or settled on a recommended solution. Knowing this, my boss had no intention of attending the meeting. Instead, he called me thirty minutes before the meeting and told me to go in his place. When I asked him what my role in the forum was and if there was anything I needed to know, I remember him saying, "Don't worry, you don't have to say anything. Just take notes. You can have my sandwich." The latter referred to the catered food delivered to these eight-hour quarterly meetings that required working through lunch.

The first PowerPoint slide shown on the day of the meeting required a response from Human Capital and EEO. There was a pecking order for where folks sat at the conference table. The V-shaped table, large enough to seat between twelve and fifteen people on each side, expanded outward from where the agency director sat at one end. Near her sat the agency's general counsel on one side, with her deputy director on the other side. The seating then filtered downwards, with all the senior executive service members sitting in a pre-determined order of precedence. Near the end, farthest away from the agency head, sat the Director, Office of Diversity and Inclusion (D&I), and the Director of Equal Employment Opportunity (EEO), both general schedule (GS)-15 positions.

The Director of Human Capital quickly shifted the blame from her on the issue at hand. The LTG then shouted, "D&I and EEO, speak up! I have you in here for a reason!" The D&I Director, sitting to my left and closer to the agency director, turned his head to the right towards me and where my boss would have sat. All eyes were now on me!

At one time or another, all of us have had or will have a defining moment. What I said next would establish me as a competent subject matter expert or someone who added no value to the discussion and would no longer receive an invite to these meetings from that day forward. I answered the General's question by providing her with options and a recommended way forward. I did so without any one-upmanship or throwing anyone under the bus. The General responded by asking, "Who are you again?" I replied, "Ma'am, I am Clint Covert, Deputy Director, EEO." Over time, the Lieutenant General would rely on me as one of her trusted advisors for all matters relating to EEO.

Near the end of her tenure, I gave her an EEO status update in her office. The discussion oscillated between current projects, requiring her awareness of pending matters that needed her final decision before departure. Sometimes, the meeting felt like part of an exit interview, even though I was not leaving the organization. I shared with her some of my frustrations with missed opportunities and my short- and long-term plans. At the end of our conversation, she said, "Clint, you always said the right thing." I knew what she meant. The Director was referring to the quarterly senior leaders meeting.

At times, these meetings would become contentious and digress at certain junctures. As a result, I would witness all types of dysfunctional behaviors, including senior leaders talking over one another, underhanded personal slights, and others withdrawing from the conversation altogether. Sometimes, something needed to be said, albeit not necessarily by the boss, to get the group back on task. While I appreciated her acknowledgment of my role in bringing everyone back into focus by saying "the right thing," I have increasingly understood the importance of active listening.

It was actively listening to what was and was not being said that led to me being able to formulate what to say to get the group back to performing the task at hand. However, as a leader, sometimes, just as critical as knowing what to say is knowing when to say nothing at all!

Johari Window

At the end of my time at one of my jobs, I was one of the guests of honor for a hail and farewell ceremony honoring those of us departing from the organization and welcoming newcomers aboard to the unit. The format included invites sent to the guests' families and friends, co-workers, and leadership team members. The agenda for such events followed a consistent plan.

Folks would meet at a prescribed date and time at a local eatery with a buffet-style dinner to follow. After eating, the expectation was that the leader would make some opening remarks, welcoming everyone with a brief overview of current happenings within the organization. The leader's comments then shifted to noting those in attendance as newly assigned personnel to the garrison. The speaker would then call each departing employee and their spouse to the front of the venue to make personal remarks and thank them for their contributions. These affairs were always lighthearted, with many things said in jest.

Leading up to this event, I thought a lot about what I would say to those in attendance when it was my time to speak. I had worked with most of them for the past seven years. Over this time, I assumed they thought they had come to know me well. So, I decided to tell them things they did not know about me rather than giving typical

41

comments associated with such events, filled with thank you remarks and rehashing past experiences. What I said to them that night had some in the audience hysterically laughing while others looked aghast in disbelief. While applicable here, a central part of this story is captured further in Chapter 7.

Below, I describe what happened before my remarks that night. It highlights how the Johari window is a tool for understanding how we view ourselves and how others perceive us. As illustrated in Figure 2, this paradigm consists of four quadrants: 1) Things we know about ourselves that others also know; 2) things we know about ourselves that others do not know; 3) things others know about us that we do not know about ourselves; and 4) things we and others do not know about us.

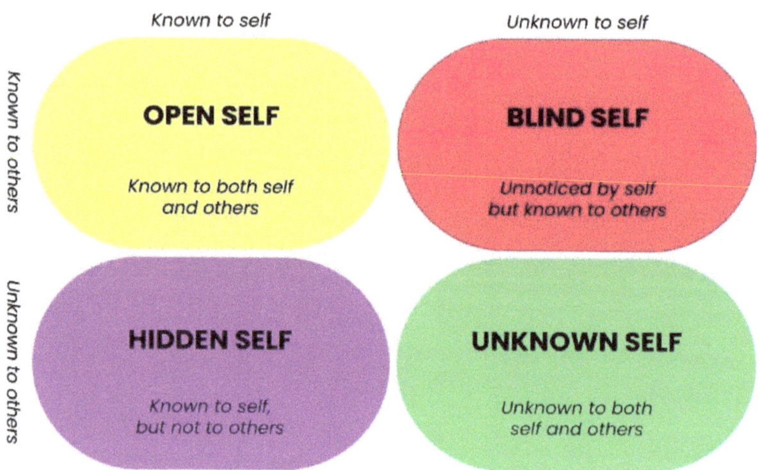

Figure 2

Source: Luft, J. *Group Processes: An Introduction to Group Dynamics* (2 ed.). Palo Alto, California: National Press Books, 1970.

Developed by Joseph Luft and Harrington Ingham, the word "Johari" is derived from the beginning of their first names, Joe-Harry or Johari, window. There are two fundamental principles behind the tool: 1) Individuals can build trust between themselves by disclosing information, and 2) individuals can learn about themselves and come to terms with personal issues with the help of feedback from others. The first factor involves what you know about yourself. The second factor relates to what other people know about you. The model works using four quadrants. First, your open area is what you know about yourself and willingly share with others. Sharing more information about yourself with others builds trust.

Things you do not know about yourself but that others see about you are your blind area. This area is how others perceive you. Being receptive to feedback from others about your positive and negative traits provides opportunities for personal growth.

Any aspect of yourself that you are aware of and that you do not want others to know is your hidden area. The final area encompasses unknown things to yourself and others and is labeled as the unknown. The balance between or the size of each quadrant can change through sharing more information about yourself, soliciting feedback from others, and self-reflection.

The third quadrant, unnoticed by self but known to others, exemplifies what happened next at my hail and farewell. Because the colonel in charge of the event that night had only recently taken command of the organization, I assumed his remarks about me would be short and somewhat superficial. I reasoned that he did not know me enough to make substantial or substantive comments since we had only interacted once or twice.

We have all heard something along the lines of "many truths are made in jest." With my wife standing alongside the colonel and me, he said, "Clint is the type of guy who has never walked past a mirror he didn't like." The crowd erupted in laughter. Shocked, I turned toward the colonel with my head tilted as if to say, "I can't believe you just said that!" He then said, "I noticed earlier, Clint, that you loaded some chicken wings on your plate." I nodded as if it was true; my wife had asked me to get her some more.

The colonel asked, "Clint, did you eat any of those chicken wings tonight?" I said, "No, sir." Without missing a beat, the colonel said, "I know you didn't, Clint." Then he cupped his right hand and motioned as if running his hand through his hair, referring to the fact that I wore my hair combed straight back with the use of hair gel, and said, "I know you didn't eat any of them, Clint, because you were afraid you might get some of that barbeque sauce in your hair." Again, the crowd erupted in laughter. What he was joking about in jest was how he saw me – as someone vain or full of himself. I never viewed myself that way, but he did.

This episode made me more aware of how there are things that others know about us that maybe we do not know about ourselves. As Michael McKinney states, "What we know often blocks us from what we need to see." At the very least, the Johari window provides a model for understanding how and what impact we have on others. Over time, we are more likely to internalize this information and begin the change process when we receive the same feedback from multiple sources. As leaders, it is essential to understand what kind of influence, positive or negative, we have on those we lead.

"We need to give each other space to grow, to be ourselves, to exercise our diversity. We need to give each other space so that we may both give and receive such beautiful things as ideas, openness, dignity, joy, healing, and inclusion."

- Max DePrcc

Valuing Diversity and Creating a Culture of Inclusivity

As I write this book, Diversity, Equity, and Inclusion, more commonly referred to as DEI, has come under attack by the current administration by removing all policies and programs associated with DEI from the federal and private sectors. However, leaders cannot put their heads in the sand and wish DEI away. There is no getting around the fact that as leaders, you will lead more and more diverse individuals and teams, and to do it successfully, you must be aware of and value diversity while treating people with fairness, dignity, and respect. Administrations come and go with the policy pendulum swinging back and forth between political parties. Whether it is the Republicans or the Democrats in charge, DEI will remain imperative to effective leadership. To lead others from diverse backgrounds, we must first be able to lead ourselves by knowing who we are.

Accordingly, this portion moves us forward in thinking more about what we know and do not know about ourselves. The Johari window is one way to expand our thinking about how others perceive us, along with starting down the path of identifying our blind spots. Because all of us have limitations about what we know about ourselves and those we lead, in this chapter, I have also defined a couple of principles that push us past getting bogged down in misunderstandings during our interactions with others. Each of us is unique. Our diversity comprises multiple layers, as depicted in Figure 2 below. Akin to peeling back the layers of an onion, various internal, external, and organizational dimensions shape our internal core – our personality. These characteristics, qualities, and factors form our distinctive individual character. As Catherine Pulsifer has noted, "We are all different, which is great because we are all unique. Without diversity, life would be very boring."

FOUR LAYERS OF DIVERSITY

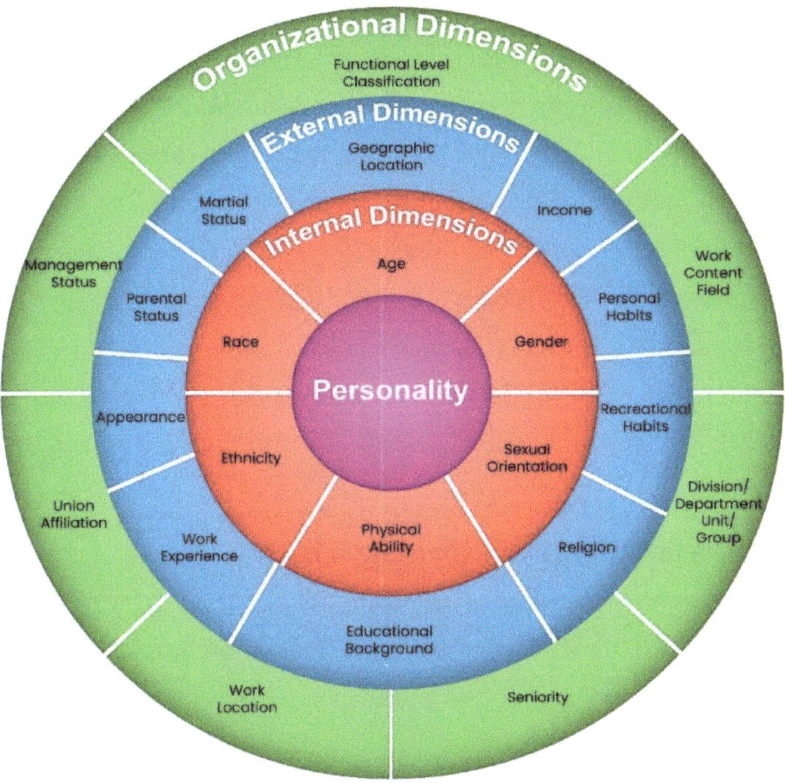

*Internal Dimensions and External Dimensions are adapted from
Marilyn Loden and
Judy Rosener, Workforce America!
(Business One Irwin, 1991)
From Diverse Teams at Work,
Gardenswartz & Rowe (2nd Edition, SHRM, 2003)*

Figure 3

As shown above, diversity is the differences in the characteristics of people. These differences include individuals' personalities, race, age, ethnicity, gender, religion, education level, and occupation. Inclusion is the extent to which everyone in an organization or group feels welcomed, respected, supported, and valued as a team member. Leadership requires leaders to combine valuing diversity and creating a culture of inclusivity by becoming inclusive leaders. In their article, *Why Inclusive Leaders Are Good for Organizations, and How to Become One*, Juliet Bourke and Andrea Espedito suggest that leadership today requires *inclusive leadership* – leadership that ensures that all team members feel they are treated respectfully and fairly, are valued, and feel that they belong, and are confident and inspired.

At the same time, by committing ourselves to be better listeners while valuing the diversity surrounding us in our workplace, we grow as leaders as we learn more about ourselves and our surroundings. In turn, we build a stronger foundation for coping with the ambiguity of leadership during a crisis.

Chapter 3 will examine the concepts of character, ethics, and ethical dilemmas. This chapter will allow you to self-reflect on questioning when or if ethics are negotiable. Further, this chapter will also raise the question of when or if the ends ever justify the means. This chapter's core builds on our ability to understand who we are better. Before moving on to the next section, take a moment to answer the questions in the below exercise.

EXERCISE

When you meet someone for the first time, what things do you focus on? Why?

____

____

____

____

What factors cause you to interact or behave differently toward some individuals? Why?

____

____

____

____

What assumptions do you make about someone based on their physical appearance, such as race, gender, dress, body type, etc.? Why?

____

____

How often are your assumptions incorrect? How does this make you feel?

What strategies have you used to overcome "blind spots" in your interactions with others?

To what extent have "blind spots" impeded your decision-making process?

____

____

____

____

How have you overcome not knowing what you don't know about yourself when leading yourself and others?

____

____

____

____

What strategies will you use as a leader to understand what you do not know about those you lead?

____

____

____

"The ultimate measure of a man is not where he stands in moments of comfort and convenience, but where he stands at times of challenge and controversy."

– Martin Luther King, Jr.

CHAPTER 3

Let Them Eat Cake

I once worked in an organization where the boss asked one of his subordinate directors to purchase a cake using unit funds to celebrate the Army's birthday. Dave, the director, refused to buy the cake. The boss followed up a week later and asked if he had purchased the cake. Dave listed a bunch of reasons why he had not done so. He believed that buying the cake would violate ethical rules and regulations. Finally, the boss said, "Dave, I have already received a legal review authorizing this purchase. Buy the cake!"

Another two weeks passed, and Dave had still not acquired the cake. Instead, he used this time to obtain an additional legal review. Dave found an attorney whose legal opinion contradicted the earlier assessment. When Dave's boss discovered this, Dave was removed from his position.

The boss, an Army colonel, and his civilian deputy commander decided to call an "all-hands" meeting for those working in Dave's unit to announce that he was no longer in his position. The Directorate, composed of over 400 personnel, appeared stunned and sat in silence when the colonel said, "Effective today, Dave is no longer the director. Ms. Johnson will now perform his responsibilities." Without further explanation, the meeting came to an end. Before this "all-hands" meeting, the colonel's deputy had called Dave into his office to tell him the news. Dumbfounded, Dave had left with his eyes glazed over and a "deer-in-the-headlights" look often associated with those forced to confront something confusing or startling.

Over the next year, Dave's new office remained empty of personal mementos. In his latest "special projects" position, nothing was hung from the walls or placed on the shelves. As a young civil servant EEO Director, I would walk by and notice Dave sitting behind his desk, staring at his laptop screen. As far as I could tell, Dave neither sought out nor was any work assignments given to him to complete. On top of this, he did not receive an invitation to attend any of the senior leader meetings. Months went by, and there Dave sat.

This public shaming led Dave to file multiple complaints. He presented one to the Equal Employment Opportunity Commission (EEOC). He recorded another with the Merit Systems Protection Board (MSPB). He followed this up by filing a third complaint with the Office of Special Counsel (OSC) in Washington, D.C. In his claims, Dave alleged his wrongful removal from his government position was for opposing unlawful actions by his supervisors. Dave conveniently omitted from his complaints that he had previously received a letter of reprimand for coercing a junior information technology (IT) specialist to give him access to his boss' email account.

Since the IT specialist resigned before the completion of the investigation to avoid having to face possible termination, further adverse actions were not taken against Dave, even though copies of the deputy commander's emails later surfaced in his office. The deputy commander was livid. The thought of a subordinate having access to his emails led to the subsequent actions that the deputy would take.

When contemplating what type of adverse personnel action to take against an employee, it is always a good practice to seek higher level buy-in for the discipline you are about to implement. In this case, the Army colonel and his deputy commander decided to inform and gain approval from the installation's senior mission commander. The top mission commander on an Army installation is dual-hatted. On the one hand, they are the Senior Warfighter focusing primarily on training and military readiness. Yet, at the same time, they are also responsible for serving as modified versions of city managers and mayors. So before going to him, the colonel and his deputy built a compelling case against Dave.

While Dave was still the director, he had multiple EEO complaints filed against him. With a directorate this size, this was not uncommon. In this capacity, Dave had to make tough personnel decisions. Inevitably, some employees did not like these decisions and lodged complaints against him, many without merit. At the time of his termination, Dave had five EEO charges against him pending in different stages of the complaint administrative process. As with all EEO complaints, the focus should never be on how many complaints a given management official has against them. Instead, it should be whether the allegations have merit or are substantiated claims.

Dave's five EEO complaints filed against him were not unusual for a directorate this size. A review of the records showed that Dave had never had a substantiated EEO complaint against him. Given these considerations, the deputy commander decided to take a different approach in building his case against Dave.

In consultation with his attorney advisor, the deputy commander asked his counsel, Mark Williams, to contact all the current complainants. He told the attorney, "Settle their cases, whatever the costs!" While mediation is a viable option for settling EEO complaints at the lowest level, many factors are involved in whether the charges can reach a negotiated settlement agreement, more commonly referred to as an NSA. A primary consideration is whether the attorney representing the agency believes the case has merit. By not settling, can the agency defend its actions as being non-discriminatory? If so, attorneys are less inclined to agree to any of the complainants' demands. The deputy's instructions to settle these cases went against the attorney's nature, with him believing the cases had no merit.

I worked with Mark for over two years as the agency's EEO Director. I recalled how two years earlier, during one EEO investigation, a complainant had screamed out to Mark, "Why don't you settle with me!!? It will cost you more to go through these proceedings with the court reporter and the cost of transcripts than if you would give me the thousand dollars I'm asking for in the first place!" Mark was unfazed by the complainant's outburst and calmly replied, "Ms. Jones, that is not the point. We are here today to establish that management has offered non-discriminatory reasons for their actions. There will be no settlement."

Shortly after the deputy commander instructed Mark to settle Dave's complaints, the five complainants came into the EEO office building separately to talk to the agency attorney about resolving their grievances against Dave. The first one asked for 5,000 dollars because of a business-based decision that Dave had approved, which led to the complainant's reduced work hours. I noted that the employee left the building about thirty minutes later, his eyes partially glazed over as if he had just won the lottery. I witnessed this dynamic repeat itself four more times in one week.

As the deputy commander had instructed, Mark reached settlements with all the cases. The problem was not settling the EEO cases; it was Mark negotiating and the deputy approving agreements more than quadruple the amount each complainant had asked for in the first place! The justification for the senior mission commander, explaining why a senior federal government employee required removal from his position, was now in place. Not buying a cake was one thing. Having multiple EEO complaints against you that cost the agency over 50,000 dollars in settlement fees was another.

Dave sat at his workstation and worked on his complaints. Over time, the agency decided that responding to all his motions took excessive time. One day, Mark called me into his office. Mark handed me an NSA that stipulated that the agency would agree to remove Dave's letter of admonishment from his personnel file if he decided to withdraw his EEO, MSPB, and OSC complaints. After reading it,

I said, "Mark, Dave is a smart guy; he is not going to agree to this." Mark responded, "I know, Clint, that is why I want you to go in there when the deputy commander presents this to him. Dave views you as an honest broker." Mark then handed me a second settlement agreement that stipulated the agency would remove the letter from his files if he only withdrew the EEO complaint. He said, "That way, when he doesn't agree to sign the first one, you can pull out this second letter and get him to agree to sign this one while he is still in the room."

My beginning relationship with the deputy commander was tenuous at best. A year earlier, the deputy had asked me, "Are you ready to join the team?" Over ten years later, this question resurfaced in my mind while watching the news about reporters questioning whether the President of the United States was obstructing justice by making veiled threats on his Twitter account. *Are you ready to join the team?* This question resurfaced with the news accounts of the President's demand for unquestioning loyalty and his placement of willing followers in key cabinet posts. When my boss asked the question, I contorted my face in confusion and responded, "What do you mean, Sir? I thought I was already part of the team."

As time passed, I always felt as if the deputy commander was trying to get a read on me, his EEO Director, about what I would and would not do. I also felt that the question had been a threat. So, I read between the lines. My boss implied that *if you want to advance in your career, you must join the program and do as I wish.*

I told Mark I was uncomfortable carrying out his plan and that it felt like a form of trickery. I then went to my boss, the deputy commander, and stated the same. While in the deputy's office, I reminded him that my position required neutrality and suggested to the deputy commander that he consider presenting the agreement to Dave another way. Around this time, a promotion opportunity had also opened up for me. From the look on the deputy's face in response to my suggestion, I was now resigned from getting the job advancement.

The deputy had decided to call Dave and me into his office and only present the second letter to him. The deputy intentionally waited until a Friday afternoon, just a few hours before Dave went on vacation for a week-long skiing trip. In his office, the deputy commander had a foot-high platform where his desk and chair sat. It was from this perched position that he looked down upon the visitors. I always assumed that this was a power play on the deputy's part. Sitting in his office, you always looked up at him with your neck pitched upward. As Dave and I sat in two chairs facing their boss, the deputy stood up from behind his desk to read the letter to Dave.

Before this day, I had never seen the deputy standing behind his desk. With the two of us seated, facing the deputy's office desk already a few feet higher off the floor, Dave and I looked upwards with our necks pitched at nearly a forty-five-degree angle. I assumed that Dave felt the power dynamic at play as well. For a moment, both of us felt "small." Dave did not agree to sign the letter stipulating the withdrawal of his complaint that day. A few months later, the deputy commander selected me for the promotion.

So, what are the lessons here? For Dave, one possible conclusion is to do what your boss tells you to do next time. Let them eat the cake! This alternative, to do what you are instructed to do, is what the decision-making authority from the OSC noted in his findings for the complaint Dave had lodged with them. However, a more pressing issue involves delving into the actions of the leaders in this scenario. This story begs the question, "Do two wrongs make a right?" In their haste to "get" Dave for not following orders, the colonel and his deputy violated ethical norms and acted unscrupulously instead of doing things by the book. The question is when or if ethics are ever negotiable. And if so, do the ends justify the means?

Great leaders' character and integrity are above reproach. They live by a personal code of ethics, whereby their actions are never in question. In knowing who we are, we do not allow our ethical conduct to go astray – ethics are non-negotiable and never used to justify our actions as a means to an end. The same is true when considering what constitutes the character of individuals. I could have quickly fallen prey to negotiating my ethical code in doing the attorney's less-than-above-board bidding to get the promotion opportunity before me. In the article, *The Psychology Behind Unethical Behavior*, Merete Wedell-Wedellsborg points out how people often do not speak up about ethical breaches because of what the author labels as *justified neglect*. In these instances, individuals remain silent because they think more about immediate rewards, such as staying on a sound footing with those in power. My character allowed me to do the hard right in the face of committing the easy wrong to get the promotion.

Knowing who we are includes a firm grasp of what we are willing or unwilling to do in a crisis. Our character and integrity guide our actions. It is our moral compass. As leaders, we will face ethical dilemmas that test our moral fabric. How we respond when faced with hard choices requires an emphasis on understanding how our character and integrity direct our paths to move beyond choosing the path of least resistance in overcoming ethical dilemmas and leadership challenges.

The words "character" and "integrity" are often misused or used interchangeably, as if both terms have the same meaning. In the following section, I explain the differences between character and integrity and illustrate how both traits are indispensable for becoming a leader that others follow willingly.

"Character is destiny."

- Heraclitus

Character

Character refers to those dominant qualities that make up an individual, such as disposition, temperament, and personality. It is further defined as the mental and moral qualities distinctive to an individual. Moral qualities or virtues include empathy, courage, honesty, and loyalty. We can all evoke a leader who lacks such behaviors or habits. At the outset of this book, we explored how our personalities are shaped by internal and external forces, beginning in early childhood. These experiences form our disposition, temperament, and mentality towards others and the world – it becomes our character. Ralph Waldo Emerson states, "The force of character is cumulative."

Character is closely aligned with integrity. You cannot have one without the other. While attending an executive education program at the Harvard Kennedy School, I had the opportunity to pose a leadership question to a former advisor of four presidents. I asked him, "In your view, what leadership trait or characteristic, if left unchecked by a leader, is the most significant predictor of their eventual failure?" Without hesitation, the advisor replied, "A lack of character!" Your character is your interpersonal interaction with others and, as Heraclitus proclaimed, your destiny.

However, as Alphonse Karr suggests, everyone has three characteristics: 1) that which they exhibit, 2) that which they have, and 3) that which they think they have. Karr's suggestion compels us to clearly define what we are willing or unwilling to do in a crisis. Our deeply held values and beliefs will prevent us from consenting to the pressures that violate our principles. Your character defines who you are – it is what you stand for.

If a character is what you are, your reputation is what you are supposed to be. Your reputation lies in the minds of others. While your wrongdoings harm your character, your reputation erodes by slanderous accusations made against you by others. As R.C. Samsel notes, "…no lasting reputation worthy of respect can be built on a weak character." Like many of you, I have experienced challenges to my reputation. As I detail further in Chapter 9, while my reputation was tested based on a single and unfounded accusation, my reputation endured throughout my leadership crucible based on my steadfast character. As Warren Bennis states, "Successful leadership is…about a set of attributes. First and foremost is character."

Closely related to the leadership trait of character is the concept of integrity. Your integrity is your consistency in private; it is how you conduct yourself when you think no one is watching. To this topic, I now turn.

"If you don't have integrity, you have nothing. You can't buy it. You can have all the money in the world, but if you are not a moral and ethical person, you really have nothing."

- Henry Kravis

Integrity

Integrity is the quality of being honest and having strong moral principles. It is the adherence to a strict personal code of moral values. Integrity is synonymous with decency, honesty, and righteousness. It is the opposite of evil-doing and wickedness. Integrity, then, is knowing the difference between right and wrong behavior.

Our actions determine if we are fair, righteous, and trustworthy. Closely related to this desired leadership trait is the concept of character. The takeaways from the above story about Dave and his failure to purchase the cake are more about examining the integrity of Dave, Mark, the colonel, and the deputy commander.

Ironically, Mark, the attorney from the above story, shared with me his dismay when one of his subordinates, another attorney, feigned being sick while taking a day off from work. Mark began to question the employee's character and integrity. He told me that his subordinate had left a voice message one day, saying he would not be coming to work due to illness. Mark said, "Clint, you have to come by my office and listen to this message; it is obvious to me that he is faking a cough." Mark said, "To make matters worse, I called him back to check on him and wish him a speedy recovery. The whole time we were on the phone, he rushed to get off. You will not believe what I heard before hanging up!" Mark was now all worked up as he mocked the voice he overheard in the background while on the phone with his "sick" employee who was supposed to be at home, "Now boarding at gate 27, American Airlines flight 1144 to Amersterdam."

The shortcomings we can see clearly in others are often missed within ourselves. Mark quickly denounced his employee's lack of integrity for lying about being sick to get an early start to his weekend. However, I observed Mark do the underhanded work of "getting" Dave without stopping to ask, "Is this the right thing to do? Is it ethical? As leaders, we must guard against the slippery slope of rationalizing in our minds that what we are doing is okay when it is not. Otherwise, we risk our moral compass being eroded over time to a point where we are void of being governed by any internal moral principles.

"The respect that leadership must have requires that one's ethics be without question. A leader not only stays above the line between right and wrong, he stays well clear of the gray areas."

- G. Alan Bernard

Ethics and Ethical Dilemmas

While character directs your destiny, ethics encompasses your identity. Ethics is a system of individuals' moral principles. This system drives our conduct when confronting right or wrong choices related to possible courses of action for a problem. Ethical dilemmas test our values when faced with situations forcing us to choose between equally undesirable options. Leadership challenges involving these stressful situations require a firm understanding of who we are to grasp the goodness and badness of the motives involved and, ultimately, the "ends" or outcomes of our actions. Ethical dilemmas raise the question of whether the ends justify the means.

There was once a senior-level civilian working on an Army and Air Force joint-base installation that would routinely badmouth the wife of a 4-star general stationed there. Ken had been working on-post for over ten years. As the director of morale and welfare activities for the assigned Soldiers and Airmen, he often met with stakeholders across the installation, including the 4-star general. During this time, Ken would see military commanders come and go as they rotated to their subsequent assignments every two to three years. This turnover led Ken to lose sight of who worked for whom.

Over time, he became increasingly resistant to supporting these 4-star commanders' desires for the type of activities offered on the installation. Ken thought he knew best. During his staff meetings, Ken would become irate when discussing new programs the current general wanted to be activated. In his office and in front of his staff, on more than one occasion, Ken would yell, "His wife is a big f*cking drunk!" when referring to the general's wife. Ken's outbursts demonstrated a lack of control and self-regulation. The example he set for those he leads was troubling. Even more disconcerting was his cavalier attitude in not recognizing that the general would inevitably find out about his rants. Soon after, the general caught wind of Ken's remarks about his wife.

First, the general sent his security detail to the military police station on-post for the provost marshal to "run" Ken's vehicle plates. Ken learned about this and protested vehemently to anyone who would listen, including me.

The general had grown tired of Ken always saying "no," mumbling reasons why something could not get accomplished. At one point, the general had stated to Ken's Army colonel boss, "When I was the corps commander at Fort Hood, if I said move the sidewalk, the f*cking sidewalk got moved! Now I have some GS-14 telling me what he will not do!" Next, the 4-star general sent one of his 1-star deputies over to see my boss, an Air Force colonel, and the wing commander.

The next day, my boss called me into his office and said, "Dr. Covert, I need you to do a command climate survey on Ken Waltman's directorate." I said, "Okay, sir, but do you know that these types of surveys from the EEO office prohibit them from being used as investigative tools?" My boss responded, "I know, but this is what the general wants." I left after telling my boss that I would get on it.

The options here for me were equally undesirable. I could choose either not to do it or be used in my capacity to author a report that would justify taking action against Ken for his demise. I decided that I would carry out my boss' order. I also decided I would not allow myself to be used as an instrument to "get" Ken. If Ken was insubordinate and foul-mouthed, there were mechanisms to address such behavior and conduct. Using the survey tool for this purpose was disingenuous. Realizing that any final report I signed would most likely end as a justification for taking action against Ken, I conducted the command climate survey. I compiled a report with recommendations to address the areas for improvement within Ken's directorate. I intentionally omitted anything construed as a justification for an adverse action from the recommendations section. I thought, "If you want to get Ken, you get him. Do not use me as a pawn to get your retribution."

My boss read the report and was satisfied. The document met the requirements – he had done as he was told to. My boss forwarded the copy I signed to the general. I could tell from the look on my colonel's face that he could see what I had done. The report was well-written and included some sound recommendations, but I could picture the general reading it and then thinking, "This report says absolutely nothing!"

Shortly after, the wing commander called Ken to inform him of the outcome of the command climate survey. He warned Ken, "Where there's smoke, there's fire." Ken retired a few months later.

This scenario shows how, as a leader, my ethics guided my actions when confronted by other leaders' ill-will intentions to achieve a personal goal. I was unwilling to be used as a medium to achieve a personal vendetta. In deciding how to respond to my boss' direction, I relied on my ethics to devise a strategy that would meet his requirements while not violating my moral code.

Thus far, we have explored what makes us unique as leaders by delving into what has shaped who we are today. Next, we reflected on what we still do not know about ourselves. Then, we examined how the leadership traits of character, integrity, and ethical conduct shape our leadership outcomes and questioned if the ends justify the means. Leaders will face moral dilemmas. When we do, our reactions to them are grounded by our character, personal integrity, and ethical orientation. Knowing who we are will serve as our foundation for reacting to leadership challenges in a principled manner.

Part 2 of this book focuses on answering why someone should follow you as their leader. Chapter 4 covers how identifying and being authentic makes others want to follow you as their leader. Chapter 5 explores the importance of leading with humility, and Chapter 6 shows how giving second chances plays a central role in leaders helping others become who they are supposed to be. But first, take a moment to answer the questions in the exercise given below.

<u>**EXERCISE**</u>

From a leadership perspective, do the ends always justify the means? How? Why/why not?

____

____

____

____

____

In your view, are your ethics ever negotiable? How, when, and why?

____

____

____

____

Have you experienced a leadership challenge that required you to question who you were? How/why?

____

____

____

____

____

What did you learn from your leadership challenge? What would you have done differently? How/why?

____

____

____

____

What personal attributes will most likely predict how leaders will react to an ethical dilemma?

____

____

____

____

PART TWO

Why Should I Care?

CHAPTER 4

On Authenticity

Authenticity has multiple understandings. When it comes to authentic leaders, it is helpful to invoke the colloquial expression used in 1964 by United States Supreme Court Justice Potter Stewart when he said, "I know it when I see it." While authenticity is somewhat subjective or lacks clearly defined parameters, being an effective leader requires knowing who you are first. Authenticity is what you think, say, feel, and do consistently. In this chapter, I explore how authenticity is pivotal in answering why anyone would follow you as their leader.

I was once invited to provide the commencement remarks for a Community College of the Air Force graduation. After being introduced, I acknowledged those in attendance and congratulated the graduates on their accomplishments. My comments began with me joking about the advice I had received earlier in my career. I said, "My goal today is to be brief, brilliant, and gone!"

I pointed out to the graduates that while their accolades were well-deserved and something they should be very proud of, it was just the beginning of a lifelong learning journey. My remarks emphasized how their education was something they should use for a higher purposc in helping others. I also encouraged them to continue their quest for knowledge to broaden their perspectives and worldviews. My speech also warned the graduating class that with this newly acquired knowledge, their education would force them to reexamine what they believe to be true and trustworthy.

Next, I suggested that none of us can see our future, and their education would prepare them to capitalize on opportunities that will inevitably come their way. As I spoke these words to the over 400 students, faculty, and family members in attendance, I thought, "One day, you are sitting in the crowd, and the next, here you are, standing in front of it." I then transitioned to a story about myself.

I began with a brief review of my educational pursuits to provide context for the remainder of my remarks. I told those in attendance how I left home at seventeen, just four days after high school graduation. I described being at Army basic training at Fort Jackson, South Carolina, and how I could not see then what I would come to experience over a twenty-year Army career. I lamented how I would not have believed it if someone had told me then that I would go to class in the evenings after work and graduate from the University of Southern California with a doctorate in higher education before retiring from active duty.

I followed this by suggesting that one of their education outcomes would be realizing just how much they still do not know. I also highlighted that they would continue to face barriers and obstacles in their future educational pursuits. I told my story to inspire them to confront and overcome these hurdles.

My commencement remarks then turned to a discussion about how their sacrifices demonstrate an ability to persist and delay gratification to achieve what is important to them. Recognizing that those in attendance would remember very little from the speech that day, I concluded by telling them another story to emphasize the most important point I wanted to get across.

I explained how I always told my staff members at work that someone was always watching them. When I said this to my subordinates, it reminded them to carry themselves professionally because you never know who is watching. For the graduates that day, I said, "Remember, someone is always watching you too! Someone is always watching you, whether a spouse, child, co-worker, peer, or subordinate."

For this audience, I suggested that they would be watching them as they continued their educational pursuits. I concluded by stating, "In life, you may never know what positive impact you have had on another individual by the example you have set with your educational achievements, but someone will always be watching you just the same."

The next day at lunchtime, I was reading a newspaper at the air base library when a young Airman came over and stood nearby. He said, "Excuse me, Sir, I just wanted to thank you for your remarks yesterday at the graduation ceremony. I appreciated what you said." I responded, "Well, thank you. I am glad to hear that." We talked for a few minutes longer. I asked him about himself and where he worked at Joint Base Langley-Eustis. The Airman said, "What you said yesterday about someone always watching you is so true. I would see you on base and observe you at different places. I would wonder who you were and what you did. I would observe how you carried yourself. I was watching you!"

As a leader, you are defined not by what you say but by what you do. You can tell someone who you are, but your words must match your actions. Knowing who you are will ensure that your actions align with your words. Knowing who you are will also predict why you do what you do and when you do it. Finally, knowing who you are grounds what others think of you; it is why they will follow you as their leader.

I once watched someone in a leadership position spend excessive time asking his soldiers which military schools they desired to attend. At face value, this could be viewed positively, that the leader's focus was on developing those in his charge. However, instead of growing his subordinates, he would hold this information over their heads as leverage for them to submit to his every whim. Again, as a leader, someone is always watching you. This person was not a leader.

Having watched his modus operandi over time, when he stopped by my office one day to ask me about my goals, I responded, "I have none." He became agitated and said, "What do you mean? I thought you were working on your doctorate!" I said, "I am, but other than that, I do not have any other goals." He looked at me dumbfounded. Becoming more frustrated, he left.

I did not tell him that my doctorate would require me to spend the summer semester living in the dorms on the campus at the University of California. My attendance would also mean gaining approval to be away from work for over three months. With this information, this individual would have become a roadblock for me to achieve this goal. He would have used it as leverage against me, and I decided to find another way to accomplish this. My brigade commander, an Army colonel, provided the means.

As the time came to register and commit to the summer residency in Los Angeles, I went to my commander. I said, "Sir, as you know, I am working on my doctorate, and part of the program involves my attendance on campus for three months during the summer. I must do so to meet all of the program's requirements before graduating." As I continued, explaining, "I am going to submit a leave request for 90 days," the colonel motioned with his hand for me to stop. He asked, "Sergeant Covert, why would you want to do that?" To mask my bewilderment at what he had just asked, I restated what I had explained when he interjected, "No, my question is, why would you want to take all your leave for that? Check with my S1 and find out the total number of days I am authorized to give you as permissible leave. That way, you will not use all your leave at once." My leader allowed me to attend the program and granted me 60 days of permissible, or "free," leave!

No one accomplishes anything of significance without the help of others. As leaders, we can either inhibit or facilitate others' success. Authentic leadership is the latter, as exhibited by my brigade commander. A year after this, I witnessed his ability to lead the brigade through a tragic helicopter mishap that resulted in the deaths of multiple soldiers. In a crisis, everyone looks to the leader. Followers demand consistency from their leaders. How leaders react during duress sets the stage for how the organization does or does not move forward. The point is that all of us will face obstacles and barriers to our pursuits. As leaders, we must build human capital to navigate these roadblocks while recognizing that it will often require the help of others. Acknowledging this requires humility.

Finding a way to complete my residency requirement was not the first obstacle I overcame to realize my educational goals. I was on a one-year hardship tour in South Korea eight years earlier. My wife, Marian, and I had gotten married a couple of months earlier when I received notification in the form of military orders directing me to this next assignment. As newlyweds, neither of us was looking forward to this twelve-month separation.

I told her, "I will make the most of this assignment. All I will do over there during my time off is attend college. Working on getting my degree will help me pass the time." Marian agreed, "Clint, I'm going to get a part-time job here in town while you're away." Because we were starting our married lives together, we also wanted to start saving for our future. Before I left for Korea, Marian and I agreed on a strict budget. By living in the barracks with all my spare time taking college courses, I lived off fifty dollars a month.

My wife and I stuck to our plan. Twelve months later, I returned from Korea one class shy of an associate in arts degree from the University of Maryland. This accomplishment was not without its obstacles and barriers. Registering and taking courses on weekends or evenings during weekdays was not a problem. However, other required course offerings were only during the lunch hour. When I asked my supervisor, Staff Sergeant Smith, if he would approve my tuition assistance forms so that I could take courses at lunchtime, he initially said no. When I asked him why it mattered what I did during my lunch hour, he paused and inquired, "What time is the course?" I responded, "The lunchtime courses run from eleven-thirty to one o'clock." Staff Sergeant Smith acquiesced and approved my request with one stipulation: "Sergeant Covert, you can take a college course, but you better be back here at work by thirteen hundred hours."

Staff Sergeant Smith knew the education center's location, slightly under a mile from our worksite. Korea, being a hardship tour, he also knew that the only transportation I had was my own two feet. He also knew that he had the authority to modify my work hours to accommodate this request and that no mission requirement required me to be back at work strictly by one o'clock. I agreed to his terms. To return to work by his cutoff, I left class early each day to run back up the hill. My professors did not appreciate me cutting class before the end of the scheduled time, and my grades in my lunch hour course suffered accordingly. It was an obstacle to overcome and a price I was willing to pay.

On the weekends, I would sometimes stop by Staff Sergeant Smith's room in the barracks. We would talk about our careers in a mentor-mentee relationship. He always shared whatever he was eating if he was snacking on something. He was recently divorced, and over time, I believe he grew tired of me lovingly talking about my wife. When I shared with him how Marian and I discussed the sacrifices we would make during our time apart, including getting second jobs, going to college, and living off a strict budget, his face soured. I told him how I was living off a budget of fifty dollars a month.

A week later, I stopped by Staff Sergeant Smith's room. I asked him for some grapes sitting in a bowl atop a small desk. Up until now, Staff Sergeant Smith had always responded with something along the lines, "Sure, go ahead." On this day, he said, "They will cost you five cents each." He was not joking.

Being in a leadership position does not make one a leader. Real leaders get to know those they lead. They do so to make those they lead better. Leaders know that it is no longer about them and that their position is sacred. I wonder if these individuals in leadership positions with authority over others ever asked themselves, "Who am I?" I suspect not. If they did, what would they say? I also wonder if they would like the answer while looking at themselves in the mirror.

Reflecting on these experiences further, I question whether these leaders ever wanted to change how others viewed them or if they even cared. I watched them go about trying to use their subordinates' aspirations against them and be an impediment to their personal growth. I quickly surmised that they were not people who displayed the type of characteristics that would lead me to view them in the affirmative when answering the second question from the title of this book – "Why should I care?"

Why would others want to be led by you? Explain.

____

____

____

____

____

As their leader, why would/should they care enough about you to willingly follow you? Explain.

____

____

____

____

What type of leader would you follow? Describe this leader's traits, characteristics, and other qualities.

____

____

____

____

____ 82

What are the similarities and differences between the type of
leader you would follow and how you have described yourself and
the kind of leader others would follow? Explain.

____

____

____

____

____

From a leadership perspective, what is your purpose? Please
explain.

____

____

____

____

____

What is your purpose? Please explain.

____

____

____

____

Does your professional purpose align or interconnect with your personal purpose? How? If not, why?

____

____

____

____

CHAPTER 5

On Humility

I retired from the Army at Fort Huachuca in Sierra Vista, Arizona. Fourteen years earlier, Marian and I had been married here. As the time neared for us to move out of our government housing and begin a new chapter, my wife said hesitantly, "Clint, what are we going to do?" Until now, all we had ever known was moving to the next Army post every two or three years. We relocated five times for assignments in Korea, Germany, Texas, and Hawaii during our time together. Our travels came full circle when my last assignment was at Fort Huachuca, where she and I had first met. Since Marian had a federal government job as a civilian on the Army base, I said cavalierly, "Oh, Marian, all we are going to do is put our stuff in storage and move off-post to some cheap apartment. We won't be there long because I will get a job soon." Having been conferred with my recent doctorate, I continued, "After all, I'm a doctor!"

We moved into a cheap, partially furnished apartment outside the Army post. I began looking for a job as an equal employment opportunity practitioner. While my wife went to work every morning, I stayed in the apartment and applied for government jobs online. A month went by, and I had no job. A second month went by, and I still had no job. Three months after retiring, I got telephonic interviews for some positions I had applied to, but there was no job offer. I was becoming increasingly frustrated as each day went by. I remember at one point remarking to my wife, "Every day seems like Groundhog Day!"

My wife and I slept in a twin bed provided by the complex. Sometime during the third month in this old apartment, the broken spring in the bed pierced through and would poke me in my right kidney area while I lay on my back. When I turned over to my stomach, it would poke me in my right lower abdomen. One night, I got up from this unbearable, broken bed and went into the living room to sleep on the dilapidated couch furnished by the apartment complex. I suddenly awoke to what I thought was running water. I stared at the floor, and from the light emitting through the curtainless window, I saw our five-pound, long-haired Chihuahua standing inches from my face. While looking up at me, Brutus raised his leg and relieved himself on the front of the couch inches from my face.

The next day, I sat at the kitchen table, applying for more jobs. At one point, I looked out the window and saw a man lifting a young child into a large garbage receptacle. The kid, who I assume was the man's son, rummaged through the garbage and handed items out to his father. I later overheard them talking about getting ready to go to and sell their goods at the local flea market outside the city limits. A week later, I went outside to discover that the wheel covers on our 1996 Saturn were missing. To this day, I am sure that these covers went to the local flea market for resale.

One night, four months into looking for a job, I felt depressed. I remember asking myself, "How did I end up here? Here I am, recently retired with a doctorate, and I can't get a job! I'm living where adults make their kids go dumpster diving outside my window, and my dog is peeing on me! What happened, Clint?" Just as I had judged others in the past, I also felt like a loser.

I got a job offer shortly after this. In November 2003, my wife and I moved to Germany. We remained overseas for a little over seven years. As we were preparing to return to the States in 2010, I told this story at my farewell dinner. I noticed people frown when I mentioned the "I am a doctor!" part of the story – how many people react when put off by someone being full of themselves. As I went on, people in the audience looked puzzled, followed by nervous laughter. I sensed that they were unsure whether this story was true. As I continued, the crowd's response turned into boisterous laughter. At some point, they realized what I told them was true.

The lady who had hired me and been my supervisor these past seven years was also in attendance. I told my colleagues how I had dressed for the telephonic interviews as if I were doing them in person. For the first month, I did the interviews in a suit. During the second month, I still wore a suit, but the jacket had come off. I told them that night how my motivation had continued to dwindle as months passed with still no job. By the third month, I no longer wore a dress shirt with a tie for these job interviews. Before continuing, I glanced around the room and found my supervisor, the one who had hired me, and then said, "And Audre, I just want to tell you, by the time you had called me to do the interview that day, I was in my underwear." The room erupted in laughter.

Once everyone had settled down, I said, "I tell you this story for two reasons. First, in life, humble yourself, or life will humble you. Second, remember that no matter how bad you think things are, they can always be worse."

Before telling this story that night, I had repeatedly considered this experience. Reflecting on who I was in the past compared to who I am now, I asked myself, "What did I learn from this?" When thinking about the man and son rummaging through the garbage, I remember how all I focused on at the time was my self-pity at not being able to land a job. It was not until later that I realized their journey was much more burdensome than mine. I remember that instead of feeling compassion, I judged them. Thinking back on who I was then, I felt ashamed. The same can be said when I reflected on Brutus peeing near my head that night. I was wrapped up in my self-centeredness and unable to see that things could have been much worse. His action also told me who I was then – someone who needed more humility. Ironically, Brutus taught me this lesson: shifting my focus from myself and having more empathy for others. I think back to this event to this day. It reminds me to remain humble and fight against being self-absorbed. I do not want to have to relearn this lesson.

"Life is a long lesson in humility."

\- **James M. Barrie**

Humility

Humility plays a crucial role in becoming an effective leader. Humility comes from the Latin word *humilis*, which means low, humble, from the earth. A humble person is generally thought to be unpretentious and modest. Humility is the opposite of hubris, excessive pride that is delusional and causes the downfall of others. Along the way, many leaders lose sight of the fact that leadership is about bringing out the best in their employees instead of treating them as a means to an end.

Adopting a servant leader's humble mindset allows them to serve their employees as they explore and grow by providing tangible and emotional support as they do so - this is not to say that humility and servant leadership are about taking on a stance of submissiveness. Instead, servant leadership emphasizes that the responsibility of a leader is to provide their employees with the tools to be responsible, think for themselves, and contribute towards successful outcomes.

Humility, then, combined with self-authenticity, lies at the heart of why others will follow you as their leader. As Warren Bennis has observed, "Leaders are only ever as effective as their ability to engage their followers. Without followership, leadership is nothing."

Authenticity

Bill George first used authentic leadership to describe how successful leaders lead with authenticity. If humility is about acting like a human being, we must first reflect on and understand our core being to lead with our authentic self. Put another way, we must peel back the multiple layers of the "onion" that make each of us unique. These layers consist of knowing who we are and understanding our life story. Another layer provides opportunities to understand our strengths and weaknesses, including what motivates and drives us. Our leadership style is also shaped by what we value. Understanding your authentic self also requires recognizing your big dreams, goals, needs, and desires.

We all have a dark side, which others do not get to see. Arriving at our core self also requires knowing what our vulnerabilities are. Then, there is what others can see in us that we cannot see – our blind spots. We can overcome our blind spots by being receptive to feedback from others. Our leadership style derives from all these factors that shape our authentic selves. To lead authentically means knowing who you are – to be self-aware.

Authenticity is being comfortable in your skin and displayed by how you present yourself to the world – your attire, appearance, and body language. Trying to be someone other than themselves does not do any good. We all have the innate ability to "see through" someone faking it. As Henna Inam points out in her book *Wired for Authenticity: Seven Practices to Inspire, Adapt, & Lead,* "When we limit ourselves by being the person we "should" be, we limit our aliveness. We may achieve success but not fulfillment because we are not living out all the important truths about ourselves, truths we need to slow down to excavate." All of us respect those who are authentic. We tend to follow authenticity willingly. We tend to be dismissive or guarded with unauthentic leaders. Which type of leader are you?

As Bennis and Goldsmith have posited in their book *Learning to Lead,* becoming a leader is a process. Multiple factors and life experiences, such as those identified above, shape who we are as human beings. These forces define our character. Who we are, our life stories, values, principles, motivations, and passions push us forward in determining our leadership purpose – it is what Bill George defined as finding your "true North." Along the way, all of us must confront a competing internal narrative about ourselves.

On the one hand, we have a positive or hopeful sense of self. This "self-affirming" narrative is challenged by a "self-doubting" internal narrative laden with negative or fearful thoughts. Ultimately, each of us has to come to terms with answering which of these two narratives is real. Which one are you?

<u>EXERCISE</u>

To what degree did/does humility play in shaping who you are now in leading yourself and others?

____

____

____

____

Think of a leader who displayed hubris. Describe what impact they had on those around them. Was this individual an effective leader? Why/why not?

____

____

____

____

What is the essence of your personal "self-affirming" or positive narrative? Describe.

____

____

What is the essence of your personal "self-doubting" or negative narrative? Describe.

Which one of these narratives is real? Which one of these narratives is you? Why?

CHAPTER 6

On Second Chances

All of us make mistakes. Because we are flawed human beings, we all benefit from giving and receiving the opportunity for a second chance. Besides, what if the person needing a second chance was you? Like most of you, my story is about getting a second chance.

My first assignment in the Army was with the 32nd Signal Battalion in Frankfurt, Germany. I began my career at McNair Kaserne, a former Army Cold War-era military post in the Frankfurt suburb of Hoechst, Germany. The three-story structure, named after World War II Lieutenant General Leslie J. McNair, showed its age even back then. One day, early in 1985, I was ordered by my platoon sergeant to take two newly assigned soldiers to the central in-processing facility (CIF) near the "Abrams" military complex near downtown Frankfurt, named after General Vietnam Era General Creighton Abrams. Instead of larger, more tactically oriented trucks designed for field maneuvers and deployments, a Volkswagen van was the most commonly used for these local troop movements.

Painted a drab olive color, over 50 such "Army green" vehicles could be seen traversing across the Frankfurt military commuting area on any given day. At the height of the Army's presence in Germany during the late 1980s and early 1990s, tens of thousands of soldiers would live and work in the Frankfurt military community alone. Before the drawdowns across Germany began in the late 1990s, it seemed as though you could see more "U.S. Forces Europe" vehicle tags than German ones. The Status of Forces (SOF) Agreement and other regulations limited military vehicles for official government use only. On this day, I planned to drive the newly assigned soldiers to the CIF, oversee the issuance of their military gear, and then return to McNair Kaserne before lunchtime.

When we arrived, the lines for soldiers receiving their first tactical gear issue, or the "TA-50" issue, were extended. A two-hour process had turned into over four and a half hours. It was 1:00 P.M. when we finished, and we were hungry. Knowing that the dining facility would close before we returned to the Kaserne, I went through the Burger King drive-through at the main Frankfurt military shopping complex, even though I knew I was not supposed to. Once I ordered everyone's food at the microphone, I proceeded forward and made a slow U-turn, heading back toward the pickup window. Like most fast-food drive-throughs, the lane was narrow, with no room to turn around. At this point, the only option was to proceed forward. I was now fully committed to it.

Moving forward, I saw two men in military uniform standing outside the pickup window. Both were in military fatigues, and one held a pen and notebook. I recognized one of them as the Frankfurt Military Community Command Sergeant Major. His grade was an E-9, the highest enlisted grade for a non-commissioned officer. He was the equivalent of a city mayor's deputy in this position. As I proceeded forward, I remember mouthing to myself, "Uh Oh!" When

I stopped in front of the pickup window, he screamed, "What are you doing in a military vehicle going through a Burger King drive-through?!" I started to mumble something, but before I could finish, he yelled, "What is your name? What unit are you assigned? What is your first sergeant's number?" As I answered the sergeant major's barking questions, I briefly looked at the staff sergeant with the pen and notebook as he scribbled away. We left.

To this day, I cannot remember whether we got the food from the pickup window. And if we did, I do not remember eating any of it. I remember returning to the Kaserne, driving through the front gate, and seeing my whole chain of command waiting there as we entered the quad. My section sergeant, squad leader, and platoon sergeant met me as I opened the driver's door of the van. They bombarded me with questions about why I had taken a military vehicle through the drive-through. At some point, one of them mentioned that the community sergeant major had told them that "I had no sense of urgency" when confronted by him. I remember responding by asking, "What did he want me to do?" The only excuse I had was that having missed lunch, we were hungry. My leadership escorted me inside to the headquarters section. The other two soldiers were told to get back to work. I prepared for the worst.

Once inside the office of our command sergeant major, they proceeded to berate me further in front of him. He then asked them, "What do you recommend?" All members of my chain of command recommended that I receive Article 15 and a reduction in rank for my willful disobedience of command policy. At some point, the sergeant major raised his hand to motion for them to stop as if to say that he had heard enough. Then he said, "No, I like Covert. So, here's what we're going to do."

Instead, my punishment was spending the weekend painting new bumper numbers on all the tactical vehicles in the motor pool. When I completed this task, I painted the street curbs outside the front gate of the Kaserne. "I like Covert." When the sergeant major said these words, I was shocked. I had not thought he even knew who I was. I had talked to him several times before that day, but these conversations were short. Instead of coming down hard on me for my transgressions, the sergeant major had given me a second chance.

Shortly after, I would re-enlist at my next Fort Riley, Kansas, assignment. At this point, I decided to make the Army a career. My life trajectory would have been very different if the sergeant major had not given me a second chance. I most likely would not have made the Army my career. I would not have been on the path where I met my future wife! And I definitely would not have gone to another Fort McNair, the one in Washington, D.C., to achieve my longtime goal of being able to attend and graduate from the National War College there as a civilian. Most importantly, I would not have had the opportunity to give others a second chance in the years to follow during my military service.

In 1992, my next assignment was near Munich, Germany, and was my second tour in Europe. This time, my wife accompanied me. One weekend, Marian and I drove up to Frankfurt. I wanted to show her where I worked before we had met at Fort Huachuca, Arizona, in early 1988. When we arrived at the Kaserne, many things had changed. It was no longer a military barracks. The U.S. government had returned the facility to the German authorities. The local government had seized the opportunity to turn the massive structure located on prime real estate into a modern apartment complex.

As we peered through the compound entrance gates, the one I had entered ten years earlier while returning from Burger King, I saw playgrounds dispersed across manicured grass where the asphalt quad once was. As we turned to leave, I stared at the street curb on the cobblestone street outside the complex's entrance and could not help but notice in the chipped paint the accumulation of the many layers of different hues over the years. I said to Marian, "See this curb right here? One of these coats was painted by me." As I continued staring at the street corner, I remember saying, "I'm glad my battalion sergeant major gave me a second chance." I did not realize at this time that five years later, I would be the one in a position to help someone get a second chance.

Soon after joining the Army, I became aware of the military detention or corrections facility at Fort Leavenworth, Kansas. While in basic training, my drill sergeant would often threaten some of the trainees in my platoon with being sent there if they did not straighten up and do as instructed. I did not know until later in my military career that most Army posts at the time had corrections facilities within their confines.

One such facility I entered was a nondescript structure as I turned off from one of the main boulevards into the parking lot facing the front of the building. As a platoon sergeant, part of my duties required me to escort one of my young non-commissioned officers for processing into the facility. Earlier in the day, Sergeant Jones received six months of confinement for burglary. He would be in-processed and spend the next two months here before being moved to an out-of-state facility in Colorado, where he would serve the remainder of his sentence.

When I became aware of Sergeant Jones's transgressions, I was dumbfounded. Of all of the Soldiers in my platoon, I thought he was the least likely to get into trouble. He always came to work on time, did what he was told, and was good at what he did. Sergeant Jones was soft-spoken but a leader just the same. At work, his soldiers listened to him and followed his example.

To this day, I do not know why he broke into other soldiers' vehicles late at night to steal car stereos. Before getting caught, military criminal investigation agents spent months tracking down the culprits for the thefts on the post. The agents scoured the local pawn shops for months to match serial numbers to the reported stolen audio systems.

One night, around 1 a.m., the military police drove up on an individual standing beside a white Volkswagen Jetta. When they asked Sergeant Jones what he was doing, he was evasive. First, Jones nervously told the police officers that the car was his. Then, he changed his story and said the Jetta belonged to a friend. When the military police (MP) asked him to open the vehicle, he could not. Jones then offered a false name when asked for his identity. Sergeant Jones was subsequently apprehended.

Next, the police went to his on-post housing. There, they found car audio systems strewn throughout his living quarters. As one of the police officers was checking serial numbers on some of the equipment, Sergeant Jones admitted to the MPs that he had stolen all of it from cars on the installation.

I drove him to my house to have lunch on the day Sergeant Jones was to go to prison. The next three hours were to be his last moments of freedom. Sergeant Jones told me, "Sergeant Covert, man, I don't know why I did what I did." I remember telling him this was not the end and that he could overcome this once he had paid his dues for the crimes. I remember feeling terrible for his wife and five-year-old son. Earlier that morning, I had taken Sergeant Jones back to his dwelling to pack the required items from the list provided by the detention facility. When we arrived, his wife and son were crying. She and the kid were returning to their hometown, Cleveland, Ohio, with no Army benefits.

A few hours later, I had to drive Sergeant Jones back to the installation and escort him inside the jail. Before getting into my car, Sergeant Jones asked me, "Sergeant Covert, when this is all over with, and I have served my time, would you mind if I listed you as a reference for when I start looking for a job?" I replied, "No, I don't mind at all."

Once inside the facility, Sergeant Jones was directed into a small restroom at the end of the hallway. There was barely enough room to maneuver without brushing up against one another. Having never escorted someone to a detention facility, I left the room. I reasoned that I was no longer required to be present for whatever would happen next. As I left, the cadre member shouted, "Sergeant Covert, where are you going? You need to stay right here!" I turned and went back inside the room. For the next 30 minutes, the officer barked at Sergeant Jones, giving him instructions on which pieces of his Class A dress uniform to remove next.

After he had taken off his jacket, folded it as instructed, and laid it on the sink counter in front of him, the detention NCO said, "Too slow!" He picked up the jacket and tossed it on the floor. "Now, pick it up, do it again!" he barked. On and on this went as Sergeant Jones was systematically instructed to remove each article of clothing until he was standing naked, except for his "Class A" uniform's patent leather shoes. Earlier in the process, he was told to remove the shoelaces for his "own safety." The inhumanity of this process was surreal.

I remember thinking that if anyone were to witness this for themselves, they would think twice before committing a crime. Once Sergeant Jones was in-processed, I was "released." I left. In the following couple of weeks, I returned a few times to bring him some authorized toiletries. Sergeant Jones was eventually transferred to the Colorado facility. I never saw him again. Eight or nine months went by when, one day, I received a call from a woman considering Jones for a job somewhere in California. She stated that he had done well on the interview, and she was now doing a follow-up with me as one of his references. My mind started to race about my response if she asked me if I knew of any disciplinary problems involving Sergeant Jones.

I decided that if asked, I would answer truthfully. If not, I would not volunteer information about Jones' criminal past. I believed that he deserved a second chance. The lady asked, "Can you tell me what type of worker Sergeant Jones is?" I told her, "While he worked for me, he was one of my best Soldiers." She asked a few more questions about his work experience as it related to the job he was in consideration for at the time. After answering these questions, she asked, "Can you tell me if he could be counted on to show up on time and if he works well with others in a team setting." I responded by restating some of his accomplishments while assigned to my platoon. I said, "I believe Sergeant Jones will excel if given this opportunity." She never asked questions about his criminal past, and I did not volunteer the information. There are certainly consequences for our actions. But I have received many second chances in life and believe Sergeant Jones deserved a second chance, too. Second chances matter – for me, you, and those we lead.

In Part One of this book, we explored what makes us unique as a leader by delving into what has shaped who we are today. Next, we reflected on what we still do not know about ourselves. Then, we examined how the leadership traits of character, integrity, and ethical conduct shape our leadership outcomes and questioned if the ends justify the means. When leaders face ethical dilemmas, their reactions are based on character, personal integrity, and moral orientation. Knowing who we are serves as our foundation for reacting to leadership challenges in a principled manner.

Above, we have extended the discussion from Part One of this book to move towards leading with authenticity. In Part Two, we examined how finding and leading with our authentic self requires resetting how we interact with ourselves and others through reflection to become more self-aware. This exploration reveals how and why others will follow you as their leader. Part of being authentic involves leading with humility. Humility plays a significant role in understanding why those you lead deserve a second chance. Because learning and growing include making mistakes, humble leaders acknowledge their past and current shortcomings while affording those they lead opportunities to overcome errors and become who they are supposed to be.

So far, this book has focused on answering who you are and why someone should follow you as their leader. To be sure, leading with authenticity means being true to yourself. It also means leading with humility. All of us have been benefactors of being afforded a second chance. Giving second chances plays a central role in leaders helping others become who they should be. It is also why others will follow you as their leader.

The final section of this book, Part Three, combines what you now know about yourself with a better understanding of why others would follow you as their leaders. Chapter 7 outlines the role competence, commitment, accountability, and building and maintaining trust play in leading others. Next, Chapter 8 implores us to shift our focus away from ourselves and toward those we lead. Then, in Chapter 9, we apply what Daniel Goldman defined as Emotional Intelligence (EI) in overcoming our leadership crucibles. In Chapter 10, I describe one of my leadership challenges to show how all the elements covered in this book are connected to effective leadership. My example also shows how leaders can fail when these elements are absent. But first, take a moment to answer the questions in the exercise given below.

<u>**EXERCISE**</u>

How has someone given you a second chance shaped who you are today?

____

____

____

____

____

Have you ever given someone a second chance in your life? If so, what impact has this had on who you are today?

____

____

____

____

____

PART THREE

Learning to Lead as You Have Never Led Before

CHAPTER 7

On Leading

As Sartre notes, the sum of its parts determines the effectiveness of a team. When an individual does not work in tandem with the rest of the team, the group cannot realize its full potential. What was true in Sartre's time remains true today. There are many ways in which a leader can respond to an individual "rocking the boat." Getting the team back on course and "rowing" in unison will require the leader to take action. The type of activity the leader chooses is directly related to their values, personality type, and leadership style. But choices have consequences, and every action causes a reaction. As we will see below, all the options have pitfalls the leader must consider. Ultimately, the leader's choice will be driven by who they are.

In earlier times, a quick response might have been, "Off with their head!" Today, this verbal expression of correcting unacceptable behavior has been replaced with a symbolic "beheading" in the form of public ridicule or threats to coerce compliance. For the leader, this represents an option. Another response is to do nothing. Inaction is, in fact, a deliberate action. A third option closely relates to this choice. The leader can hope that the rest of the team will compel the person "rocking the boat" to modify their behavior through peer pressure. A fourth option is for the leader or "captain of the ship" to find out why the teammate is not "rowing" and persuade them that it is in their best interest to do so. A fifth choice is for the leader to hold the "deckhand" accountable.

When I was in the Air Force's Air Staff and Command College, the capstone event involved planning and executing a strategic air campaign against a fictional enemy. For this exercise, you had to understand the proper aircraft to include in building the strike packages. As the campaign planner, I also had to follow the Commander's intent. Other considerations were the enemy's strengths and weaknesses in relation to my logistical capabilities. The most important concept was forecasting the second-and-third-order effects of the bombing campaign. The campaign strikes (actions) would have short- and long-term impacts (reactions) upon the enemy force's will to fight, political forces, economic markets, and human suffering.

For the Sartre scenario above, all the options have potential second-and-third-order effects for the leader to consider. The first option, leading by fear, threats, and intimidation, may be a practical choice for the short-term, resulting in the desired outcome – the guy gets back to "rowing." The pitfall of this option is that this strategy rarely works long-term. The subject of public humiliation might lead to despising the leader. During the entire duration of their work, they do so only half-heartedly. The threatened individual might spend their day conspiring with others to sabotage and overthrow the leader or "captain."

The second option of choosing to do nothing also causes strife. In this scenario, the remainder of the team directs its condemnation toward the leader. As they row away, they despise the leader for failing to correct the disruptive behavior of the individual "rocking the boat." Again, as a leader, someone is always watching you. The inaction of the leader could lead to unrest and possible mutiny.

The third option, peer pressure, may or may not be a good choice. The risk is that peer pressure might not work. In this scenario, the team is now more divisive and dysfunctional because they try to fix the problem themselves instead of the leader confronting it head-on. In turn, the leader loses the team's respect, and productivity declines.

The fourth choice, persuasion, may be viable depending on why the individual stopped rowing. The person could be having a bad day with unresolved private matters festering inside. In this case, the leader can coach the team member back to full performance. However, this fourth option will not work for an unmotivated individual. Maybe the guy tells the "captain" he is unmotivated because he believes his compensation is inadequate. In this case, the leader trying to coax or bribe the individual by awarding additional pay will only result in an overcompensated, unmotivated employee.

There is, however, the fifth option. This option is for the leader to hold the guy accountable for not rowing to the standard and take action against him if he does not adjust and perform accordingly. Holding individuals accountable is what the rest of the team expects you to do. Too often, however, leaders lose sight of the fact that accountability works both ways. In addition to holding others accountable, leaders are also responsible for keeping themselves accountable – they are watching you, too!

Leaders must understand what motivates those they lead. However, a leader must first recognize what values drive your motivation. It is this understanding of who you are that will be a predictor of what choices you will make. These choices have consequences for those you lead and the entire organization. Understanding who you are will ensure you make good decisions and get the team to work in unison toward a common goal. The intersection of leadership and groups working toward a common goal can take many forms. Likewise, leading others can be in informal or formal settings that evolve over time and space.

For example, the next time you are on an airplane, take a moment to notice what happens before takeoff and shortly after landing. Once the flight attendants (the leaders in this context) complete their instructions for what to do in an emergency, most passengers stop conversing, and quiet befalls the cabin until the plane successfully lifts off. Similarly, many passengers clap immediately after the plane's touchdown when landing. In this scenario, the attendants lead individual strangers assembled in a tight confine to get the group to behave in a manner that results in safe travel. Like the takeoff and landing aspects of flying, life is a journey with a substantial portion of our lives spent at work. Whether rowing on a boat in earlier times, traveling on an airplane, or our daily interactions at work today, successful leaders can translate to each team member how working in unison benefits the entire group, along with the realization that we are all on this journey together.

As this scenario shows, leadership involves an ongoing assessment and re-assessment of the internal and external factors that affect individuals' motivations and groups' cohesion in being productive in accomplishing the task at hand. Just as a single definition of leadership remains elusive, no cookie-cutter answer applies to every leadership challenge. As leadership consultant Zafar Achi says, "In complex systems, there is no recipe, only art."

Instead of attempting to prescribe what a leader should be or do, working our way back from the end is helpful. One way is to ask, what type of leader would you willingly follow? Your response encompasses most of the skill sets that most effective leaders exhibit. While maybe somewhat different than mine, your answer to this question lays out the type of leader you want to be led by. At a minimum, an effective leader is competent, committed, accountable, and trustworthy. I explore these topics in further depth below.

"There is nothing which rots morale more quickly and more completely than…the feeling that those in authority do not know their own minds.."

\- **Lionel Urwick**

Competence

Competence represents a measure or level of ability to complete a task. Either you have developed the capacity to lead others or not. The transaction between leaders and their followers hinges on those being directed having the faith that the leader can lead. While someone can learn to lead, being thrust into a leadership position is not meant to discover that you lack the competence to do so.

This phenomenon is best illustrated by the concept developed by Laurence J. Peter. Known as the Peter Principle, this theory posits that within an organization, people are advanced until they reach a point or level of incompetence for the highest position they are promoted. An even more cynical take is the Dilbert principle. This concept suggests incompetent employees are propelled into management positions to limit the damage they can do. To lead others, we must first be competent in leading ourselves. We must also be willing to learn new things – it must be part of who we are. Only through our individual growth can we grow those we lead.

The same holds true in answering the second question from the title of this book – Why should I care? People will only begrudgingly follow a leader who they believe to be incompetent. A leader's positional power wanes over time when their followers view them as someone unworthy of their commitment. Just as leaders lacking competence are challenged to have willing followers, individuals are hard-pressed to follow an uncommitted leader.

Commitment

The concepts of motivation and commitment are often used interchangeably. However, there are distinct differences. Motivation is aligned with one's internal drive or desire. Commitment represents personal determination and dedication – it is a state of being emotionally attached or obligated to inspire others to accomplish the desired task. Commitment is the decision to act on what motivates you. The drive that inspires your commitment is your motivation.

Chapter 4 above began with emphasizing the importance of understanding that, as a leader, someone is always watching you. Commitment goes to the heart of many leadership facets covered in this book, such as applying sound ethics and acting with integrity. Commitment is also part and parcel of the makeup of your character. Observable acts confirm leaders with a personal commitment to themselves and those they lead. In turn, leaders' actions inspire others to become committed.

In sum, for leaders to motivate others, they must be committed to the organization, the mission, and, most importantly, to those they lead. You cannot fake commitment. We all have an innate ability to "see through" someone who is uncommitted. Followers will struggle to remain committed to the uncommitted leader.

Leaders lacking commitment are often an outgrowth of the lack of accountability – the leader is void of personal accountability while at the same time not held accountable for their unaccountability. One can surmise how this cycle quickly leads to unproductive outcomes and lower morale.

> *"It is not only for what we do but also what we do not do, for which we are accountable."*
>
> **- Moliere**

Accountability

Accountability is an obligation or willingness to accept responsibility or accountability for one's actions. Loretta Malandro notes in her book *Fearless Leadership: How to Overcome Behavioral Blind Spots and Transform Your Organization*, "You cannot take charge without taking accountability, and you cannot take accountability without understanding how you avoid it." Leaders, then, are accountable both to themselves and those they lead.

While writing this chapter, I could not help but reflect more on one of my leadership crucibles, which is covered below. In answering for myself, the question, what type of leader would you willingly follow? I quickly realized that what I listed were things that my leader was not.

As I explain in further detail in Chapter 9, my boss exhibited only partial competence - she would go out of her way not to answer questions in writing or attend higher-level staff meetings for fear of being put on the spot, exposed for her incompetence, and held accountable. She was also not committed to the organization or her staff. While she would keep those in her charge accountable, she did not require the same accountability for herself. At the same time, the organization's senior leaders would look the other way instead of confronting her. Finally, her conniving and manipulative disposition made her untrustworthy.

"Trust is the glue of life. It's the most essential ingredient in effective communication. It's the foundational principle that holds all relationships."

- Steven R. Covey

Trust and Trustworthiness

In his book, *The SPEED of Trust: The One Thing that Changes Everything*, Stephen Covey states,

There is one thing that is common to every individual, relationship, team, family, organization, nation, economy, and civilization throughout the world—one thing which, if removed, will destroy the most powerful government, the most successful business, the most thriving economy, the most influential leadership, the greatest friendship, the strongest character, the deepest love. On the other hand, if developed and leveraged, that one thing has the potential to create unparalleled success and prosperity in every dimension of life. Yet, it is the least understood, most neglected, and most underestimated possibility of our time. That one thing is trust.

The same holds true for trustworthiness as well. During my doctorate studies, my dissertation chair, University Professor Bill Tierney, repeatedly said, "Clint, show me. Don't tell me." His point was that I needed to convince the reader that the data I presented and my dissertation's findings were trustworthy. My study included survey questionnaires, individual and focus group interviews, and personal observations. This data triangulation aimed to show the reader how my study's conclusions and recommendations could be deemed trustworthy. In the realm of leadership, trustworthiness refers to someone reliable. Trust occurs over time through repeated demonstrations of truthfulness and reliability.

Leaders also set the conditions for a favorable organizational climate. Organizations lacking trust resemble Franz Kafka's *The Castle,* where uncertainty and an unresponsive bureaucracy run rampant. No one is held accountable for their actions or inactions in this environment. Without accountability, no one can be counted upon to do what is right.

Therefore, the alignment of leaders' words and actions is paramount. When there is a chasm between what a leader says and what a leader does, this incongruence in behavior leads to mistrust. A lack of trust erodes employee morale and productivity. As mentioned above, all leaders have a responsibility to be accountable for their actions.

When conflict arises in the workplace, the root cause often leads to a lack of trust between supervisors and employees. Few would argue that trust is the foundation of any personal relationship. Initial trust is how a relationship starts, and it is through the development of trust that the relationship grows. No relationship can survive without trust. As soon as there is a breakdown in trust, the relationship deteriorates, and there is conflict. Likewise, matters of trustworthiness are paramount to a healthy state of being, given that we spend approximately a third of our adult life at work.

Trust means to believe. When you extend your trust to someone, you do not doubt the other person's honesty, integrity, and credibility. Integrity is the quality of being honest and always upholding the highest standards of ethical and moral behavior. Service is showing up and being committed to your work as a public servant for the nation's benefit, putting professional responsibilities before self-interests. Excellence is your actions in doing your best each day in everything you do. When individuals do not adhere to these principles, trust breaks down.

Any break in trust creates problems. In the absence of the restoration of trust, the relationship will dissolve. To build and maintain trust, you have to be trustworthy. If you are not dependable, you will doubt the trustworthiness of those you work for or lead. Trust acts as the cement of your foundation. If it starts to crack or crumble, your relationships at work will be unstable. So, ask yourself, do you trust your leader? Leaders, do you trust your employees? If not, why? What are you doing or not doing that has caused this rift between you and those you lead?

<u>EXERCISE</u>

For the scenario above, which option would you choose for the "guy who isn't rowing? Why?

____

____

____

____

Have you experienced a leader who chose one of the other options listed to influence someone to accomplish a task? Was the leader successful? Why or why not?

____

____

____

____

Have you worked under a leader who was over their head, beyond their capabilities? Describe this environment and how you coped with the situation.

____

____

____

____

____

What significance do competence and accountability play in being a successful leader? How and why?

____

____

____

____

As a leader, how do you inspire trust in those you lead?

____

____

____

CHAPTER 8

What About Me? It's No Longer About You

We spend our early years as infants with other people caring for our every need. We are fed, bathed, and fawned over by parents, grandparents, aunts, uncles, and other family members. It is all about us during this time; that is how it should be. As we grow physically and mentally with age, we transition from having others care for us to becoming responsible for managing ourselves. Not only do we take control of our physical well-being, but we also become responsible for making decisions and living and learning from our choices.

As leaders, these same dynamics take place. To be an effective leader, we must move from a mental state that focuses solely on ourselves to one that prioritizes the needs of others. This shift in focus leads to the personal growth of those in your sphere of influence. It is also a recognition of knowing who you are and an acknowledgment by those you lead of why they care enough to follow you as their leader.

The guest speaker for my Executive Leadership Development Program graduation drove this point home. I do not remember the substance of most graduation speeches. For me, takeaways from remarks of this type are limited. However, this speech was different. It resonated with me because the speaker ended each portion of his comments with six words that night: "It is no longer about you!"

Having read each of our professional biographies before his remarks, the speaker began by stating how impressed he was with our professional accomplishments to date. He said, "After tonight, it is no longer about you."

Some of the most powerful speeches for me have a rhythm or cadence to them, with a few takeaways repeated throughout the remarks. During my doctoral studies, my professors would say, "As an introduction, tell them what you will tell them, then tell them. And as a summary, tell them what you just told them." The guest speaker's remarks that night incorporated these elements, which have stuck with me today. In sharing this story with you, I hope to pass on a key point about leadership – the higher you ascend on the leadership ladder, the lesser it is about you. At least, that is the way it should be. No one accomplishes anything significant in life without the help of others. To acknowledge this is the first step in taking our focus off ourselves and placing it on those we lead. In the end, it is no longer about you!

My assignment was at a forward support battalion within the First Cavalry Division. Every Thursday, the mornings were blocked for non-commissioned officers to conduct training for their junior enlisted soldiers. The topics for this "Sergeant's Time" training ranged from performing preventative checks and maintenance on military equipment to creating a personal budget. My military occupational specialty, more commonly referred to as MOS, was electronics maintenance repair. My platoon worked in a building inside the brigade's motor pool, where we repaired the battalion's electronics and communications equipment.

The expectation for "Sergeant's Time" training was always the same. First, conduct it every Thursday morning. Second, make sure that everyone is present and paying attention. Finally, the training must be well thought-out, with a training or lesson plan instructed to "the standard." Too often, one or more of these things did not take place. Over time, the monotony of this training led to complacency. Mostly, there were never any consequences for conducting less-than-standard training. However, you did not want to be the non-commissioned officer in charge on the day that training was spot-checked by a senior leader, with the training having turned into what was known as a "clusterfu*k!"

One day, I was the one in charge of training. Midway through the session, the Corps Command Sergeant Major burst through the front door of our facility. At the same time, someone shouted, "At Ease!" As the sergeant major walked to the rear of the facility, where my platoon was seated in a semi-circle, he cried, "Who is in charge here?" Behind him was a small entourage of a couple of his subordinate aides and my company commander and first sergeant. I stopped mid-sentence from my training instruction and responded, "I am sergeant major." I looked past him only to see my commander and first sergeant looking like they had seen a ghost. There was fear written all over their faces with an expression that appeared to be them hoping and praying that the training was taking place, that everyone was present and paying attention, and that the training was well thought-out and being instructed to "the standard." On this day, it was.

The sergeant major instructed me to proceed with the training. The class I was giving that day was on financial planning. After another 20 minutes, he walked out without saying anything, with my company commander and first sergeant following sheepishly behind.

That evening, the commander held a company recall formation in the motor pool for the assigned 200 personnel, where he proclaimed that the Corps Command Sergeant Major had told him that he had the best "Sergeant's Time" training in the division. The commander, Captain Cooley, had taken all the credit. The next day, I was scheduled to go to Fort Gordon, Georgia, to attend a mandatory three-month advanced non-commissioned officer course (ANOC) for mid-career professional development. I forgot about this incident until I returned to the unit after completing the course.

Upon returning from ANOC three months later, one of my sergeants asked, "Hey, Sergeant Covert, did you get your coin?" I responded by asking, "What coin?" Sergeant Friedman then told me that the day after I had left to go to ANOC, the Corps Command Sergeant had returned to our facility to present me with one of his leadership coins for a job well done and in recognition of my excellent training.

Sergeant Friedman had told the command sergeant major that I was at ANOC. Since I was not there, the sergeant major mentioned that he would leave my coin with my first sergeant and commander to give to me upon my return. At first, I gave my first sergeant the benefit of the doubt. I rationalized that he had probably forgotten about it and would give it to me semi-formally during one of his subsequent recall formations. This day never came.

One night, I was the Charge of Quarters. More commonly referred to as "CQ," this duty required pulling a 24-hour shift while serving as the point of contact for all incoming calls to the unit. Bored out of my mind at 2:00 a.m., I walked through the battalion headquarters, performing my security checks. As I passed the personnel section or "S1" desks, I noticed my first sergeant's evaluation report sitting on one of the tables. The personnel specialist processing his appraisal had probably forgotten to return it to the file cabinet before going home that evening. Instantly, I wondered if he had taken credit for my "Sergeant's Time" training as my commander had done four months earlier. I found that the first sergeant had taken credit for my training and kept my coin! As I scanned the back of his appraisal, I remember my eyes widening as I read aloud, "Received the Corps Command Sergeant's Major Coin for informative Sergeant's Time training!"

As will be discussed further in Chapter 9, Daniel Goldman defines emotional intelligence in part as the capacity for individuals to become self-aware. Acquiring this self-awareness allows us to build empathy and grow more aware of others, including those we lead. At this stage, leaders move from the "I" to the "we." Instead of focusing on ourselves, we start laying the groundwork for others to succeed. It is no longer about us – the focus shifts to mentoring others to excel.

My leaders lacked emotional intelligence. Their actions caused me to hold them in low regard for the remainder of my assignment. I viewed them as self-serving opportunists who only cared about themselves. Instead of recognizing my efforts, the commander and the first sergeant had taken all the credit to advance their careers. Reflecting on this now, I only recall what my commander said in front of the company formation and what he had written on the first sergeant's non-commissioned officer report: "I had the best training in the division" and "I received the Corps Command Sergeants Major Coin for my professional Sergeant's Time training."

When I was on active duty in the Army, there was a saying that the farther away a unit's location is from the "flagpole," the more likely the unit would fall prey to poor leadership and low morale. The "flagpole" referred to where the headquarters and senior leaders resided. While stationed in Germany in 1992, my battalion headquarters was in Karlsruhe, a little over 100 miles from my signal company in the southern Bavaria part of Germany. Unbeknownst to me then, our newly assigned company commander, Captain Conway, was from the battalion headquarters staff.

Captain Conway was outside the traditional age bracket of a junior officer of his grade. Having been previously enlisted and recently passed over for promotion to the rank of major as a commissioned officer, Conway was closer in age to his battalion commander boss than his captain peers. While toiling away in a dead-end staff position at the headquarters, Conway befriended the battalion commander to no small extent because of their proximity in age and their affinity for hard drinking at military and other social events. The battalion commander would come to sponsor and endorse Conway for one more command assignment as a company commander to heighten his chances of getting promoted and remaining in the Army.

Given his penchant for having a drinking buddy or two, it was unsurprising when Conway singled out a couple of senior non-commissioned officers to drink with on the weekends shortly after taking command. This fraternization with a few enlisted officers soon created strife and distrust within the unit. Over time, Conway's shenanigans would escalate due to an "I can do anything I want" or "I am above the law" mindset, given his close friendship with the battalion commander and our unit being over a hundred miles from the headquarters.

One day, one of his enlisted drinking partners came under investigation for allegedly assaulting his wife with a knife. Shortly after, his other drinking partner was caught driving under the influence and arrested by the local German police. As Captain Conway's personnel security non-commissioned officer, one of my responsibilities was to forward derogatory information to the Central Clearance Facility (CCF) at Fort Meade, Maryland. As the Army's executive agency for personnel security determinations in support of Army 0worldwide missions, they would then determine if the infraction warranted the individual's security clearance revocation. Almost everyone assigned to our unit required top-secret security clearances for the work conducted at the military facility. The sensitivity and importance of whether someone's clearance was revoked or temporarily suspended were to guard against someone being prone to blackmail. Captain Conway called me into his office and said, "Sergeant Covert, I am giving you a direct order. Do not forward the derogatory information about Staff Sergeant Finch." I did not follow this order; it went against Army regulations. I sent the report by certified mail to Fort Meade the next day – it was my job.

Around this time, Captain Conway called me to express his frustration about how the investigation against Sergeant First Class

Hooks for attacking his wife had reached a standstill. The criminal investigation unit was getting ready to close the case. Sergeant Hook's wife said that an unidentified assailant had snuck up behind her while washing clothes in the basement of the housing complex where they resided. Her husband denied any involvement. With the evidence pointing toward SFC Hooks having attacked his wife, the investigators grew increasingly frustrated each day with Mrs. Hooks's unwillingness to identify her husband as the culprit. When the investigators could not get SFC Hooks to sign a sworn statement admitting his guilt, Conway put his next planned course of action into motion. He instructed me to drive SFC Hooks to see an Army psychiatrist. He told me in his office that he hoped that SFC Hooks would let his guard down and admit to stabbing his wife to the Army doctor or me while at the hospital.

On the drive up to Wurzburg, SFC Hooks told me Captain Conway was doing everything he could to end the investigation. I could see how SFC Hooks would have come to believe this, given that he was one of Captain Conway's drinking partners. While driving, I thought about how his interpretation of Captain Conway's intentions differed significantly from what the commander had told me. Conway intended to trick him into admitting to stabbing his wife. At some point, I said, "Sergeant Hooks, I do not think Captain Conway has your best interests, and I am going to leave it at that."

In addition to having a penchant for drinking with a few non-commissioned officer subordinates, Conway also enjoyed playing in an amateur German-American rugby league. One weekend, he drove to Manheim, Germany, on a Saturday to participate in a game. I suspect he enjoyed playing rugby primarily because of the heavy drinking that followed the matches. While returning to his military housing, Conway sideswiped a local German national's car while cruising down the autobahn at over 90 miles per hour. Instead of pulling over to assess if the lady in the other car was okay, he sped up and continued to race back home to his government housing. After swerving off the side of the autobahn, the German driver regained control of her car and had the composure to record Conway's license plate. Realizing that Conway would not stop, she gave up the chase and called in his vehicle plate to the German police.

A couple of hours later, Conway's car sat parked in his assigned parking space at the community housing where he resided with his wife when a couple of German Polizei and two military police officers knocked on his door. His wife answered the door and explained that her husband was napping. At the request of the policeman, she awoke her husband. As the German and American police waited at the door, they glanced toward Captain Conway's car. The entire passenger side showed scrapes and dents from the front fender back to the rear taillight. Its condition was more like that of a car after a highly contested NASCAR race than a passenger vehicle; it also showed streaks of silver paint from the German car.

Conway came to the door and defiantly explained that he had been at his house all day. As he talked, the policeman could not help looking back over their shoulders at his car. Also evident was a large puddle of fluids leaking from underneath the engine compartment. One of the military police officers asked Conway to submit to a blood-alcohol test. The Status of Forces Agreement, more commonly referred to as the "SOFA," between Germany and the United States, allowed German authorities to have jurisdiction since this incident involved a U.S. Soldier damaging the property of a German national on a German highway.

Conway became increasingly agitated and, at one point, pointedly asked, "Do you know who I am?" Then, one of the young American patrolmen said, "Look, you can either consent to have your blood drawn, or these two Polizei will take it forcefully. Either way, they are getting your blood!" The results revealed that Conway's blood-alcohol level was twice the legal limit despite taking the test three hours after sideswiping the German car. Conway's apprehension was the beginning of the end of his military career.

On Monday morning, the senior leaders at the "flagpole" became aware of Conway's transgressions. Since taking over, the new battalion commander had heard rumblings of Conway's poor leadership and toxic command climate. The battalion commander summoned Conway to her office. The lieutenant colonel commander told him, "I am removing you from your position as a company commander for my loss of confidence in your ability to command based on your recent actions and violations of the Uniform Code of Military Justice." Before separating him from the military, she directed him to self-enroll in a 30-day residential treatment facility in Rota, Spain, for his drinking problem. The battalion commander had decided that the $30,000 cost was worth it if it meant that she could play a part in getting him help to fix his drinking problem.

A couple of weeks after completing the program, Conway was seen sitting at a table at a local Oktoberfest celebration. Conway would be out-processed in a few weeks, flown back to the United States, and separated from the service. As a local German band played, he sat with Staff Sergeant Finch and Sergeant First Class Hooks as they each raised their 22-ounce beer steins and chugged the local pilsner beer.

Do you know who I am? That is the question Captain Conway had posed to the policeman. At the time, he had defiantly asked this question as if to say to the young, enlisted military member, "How dare you ask me to submit to a blood-alcohol test! I am a Captain in the Army!" His over-inflated sense of self-importance led to his demise and hitting rock bottom.

Before his missteps that led to his eventual downfall, instead of asking others, what if Captain Conway had asked himself, "Who am I?" I presume he would not have liked all the answers to this question, but his brutal honesty with himself could have led him to make some life course corrections and avoid that fateful day on the Autobahn. Our truths are sometimes harsh to swallow. For Conway, it would require acknowledging that he was misusing his command authority and that he had a severe drinking problem. He needed help. While the incoming battalion commander demonstrated the leadership attribute of compassion by enrolling him in detox for his drinking problem, Conway's actions after completion of the course confirm that as leaders of ourselves, the onus for change rests solely on each of us individually.

As these stories show, people in leadership positions lose their way when they cannot shift their focus to others. In the above examples, the leaders have either lost their moral compass or have never acquired one in the first place. Their actions speak volumes about the importance of personal integrity and character, as outlined above. It is impossible to move from a position of self-centeredness to one that focuses on improving those around them without these traits. Making others better is at the core of being a good leader. Far too often, this form of selfless service is the exception rather than the norm.

How has your experiencing toxic leadership impacted your leadership style? How and why?

____

____

____

____

____

How has your leadership philosophy changed over time? How and why?

____

____

____

____

____

Over time, as a leader, how have you shifted your focus from you to those you lead?

____

____

____

____

____

What strategies do you use to place the well-being of those you lead over your wants, desires, and concerns?

____

____

____

____

____

"Anyone can steer the ship when the sea is calm…"

– Publilius Syrus

CHAPTER 9

Leadership Crucibles0

Learning takes place in many forms. One way to learn more about leadership is by reading books about leadership theories, models, and styles. Further comprehension often occurs by reflecting on your reading to find utility and practical application. Your responses to written exercises and participation in small group discussions also aid in learning. Another way to learn about leadership is through personal observation. Every day, we have opportunities to learn by watching those around us. Doing is the third way to learn more about leading yourself and others. Many times, the lessons from personal experience stick; they are also the ones that cause the most pain and discomfort.

Crucibles are severe tests or trials. Therefore, leadership crucibles are when you are forced to confront your most significant personal or workplace challenges to persevere in overcoming adversity. Along the way, these crucibles will force you to ask, "Who am I?" The answer to the question directs your path forward. These crucibles will teach you many things about yourself. Often, the most important lessons from your leadership crucible will take place long after the challenge has ended through self-reflection. The study of leadership by doing, in the form of leadership crucibles, leads to personal growth. These tests answer the question: Who am I? What follows is one of my leadership crucibles.

We have all heard the saying, "Be careful what you wish for; you just might get it!" Moreover, most of us have experienced something in our lives where this statement has proven true. I have wished for job promotions throughout my military and civilian careers. This wish has also been granted numerous times over the past 35 years. Although I have received what I have wanted, I have come to realize that more important than getting the next promotion is getting the "right" job.

For me, there is not enough prestige in a job title or money to work in a position where I am miserable. The key is to land the right job with the right circumstances to experience self-fulfillment in leading yourself and others. I still wish for things, but now, I am particular about what I pray for and ask to receive. After all, I just might get it!

Another truism for most of us is, "If only I knew back then what I know now…" In late 2014, I wished for a promotion and received one shortly after that. For the past five years, I have thought a lot about being careful about what I wish for and have asked myself, "What would I do differently if I knew back then what I know now?" Given everything that has happened and knowing what I know now, would I still have taken the position?

On the day of my interview for the job promotion, one of the office staff members greeted me in the lobby of the building and proceeded to escort me to the director's office. As I neared the entrance, I saw him rise from behind his desk and walk towards me with his arm extended. Dr. Jones then motioned for me to take a seat. I was taken aback by how close we were sitting across from each other – our knees were touching. I remember thinking this guy must be trying to intimidate or bully me.

Skipping the traditional small talk that usually precedes the formal interview process, with a hurried tone, Jones said, "Look, I have already gone through your resume, so I have just three questions. First, tell me something I should know about you that I have not already gleaned from your resume. Second, if you were to walk through a dark tunnel and your subordinates, peers, and past supervisors could see you, but you could not see them, what would they say about you? Third, why should I hire you?" Jones's comments and demeanor throughout the interview made me conclude that he was an arrogant, self-centered narcissist. When he asked me his third and final question, my answer was short and to the point. While honest, I also believed he wanted and needed to hear it. He asked, "Why should I hire you?" Without hesitation, I responded, "Because I am going to make you look good." No more than ten minutes after entering his office, I left. A few days later, I received a notification from human resources stating that I had been selected along with the official job offer to serve as Jones's deputy.

A few months into the job, the staff member who escorted me on the day of the interview confided in me that Dr. Jones had expressed his doubt about selecting me after I had left his office on the meeting day. On the one hand, he thought I was the best candidate of all those he had interviewed. But Jones was hesitant to hire someone also with a doctorate. While he would demand that everyone address him as

"Doctor," I have never done so - only after the staff member convinced him that she was sure I understood how to defer appropriately to him as the boss did he select me.

Two weeks after I joined a new position at a new agency, Dr. Jones was suspended and placed on administrative leave while under investigation for some alleged misdeeds. I was now both the acting director and deputy director. The charges against him ranged from taking a female subordinate mattress shopping during the workday, going on daily extended lunch breaks, with some lasting over three hours, and repeatedly referring to a male subordinate as "crazy." The charges against him alleged he had created a hostile work environment due to his toxic leadership style.

I would remain the acting director for the next ten months. Also, I was expected to lead a staff that Dr. Jones had corrupted. Office morale was low. Trust was non-existent. Gossip was pervasive. Accountability was absent. At the same time, because of my recent promotion, there was no provision in the government pay system to allow me to receive a temporary promotion or salary increase for taking on these additional responsibilities.

Upon completing the investigation and before the agency's senior leader decided on the inquiry findings, Jones requested and was approved to retire. His doing so allowed him to receive his full pension. Before retiring, he could stay home and collect his full GS-15 salary for over five months. With all the additional responsibilities placed on me, I often asked myself, "Who is the one being punished here, him or me?" This paradox brings me back to the question,

"Would I have done anything differently if I knew back then what I know now?" The answer is no.

After going through this, I realized that this challenge only strengthened me. It built my capacity to overcome some of the most difficult circumstances as a leader. At the same time, it expanded my life experiences and forced me to ask myself on more than one occasion, "Who am I?" Before accepting this job, I would have immediately turned down this offer if I could have watched this scenario play out. I would have thought, "Someone else can deal with this buffoonery." However, by going through what I went through, I now know that it would have been a missed opportunity to grow as an individual and a leader. When we ask for something, we must be willing to accept everything that comes with it. In the long run, what we get only improves us.

Moreover, maybe that is why we do not know things before they come to fruition. However, this story does not end here. My leadership challenge would soon escalate with the arrival of my next boss.

Unbeknownst to me, a prior EEO Director had "return rights" to Dr. Jones's position. Although he knew that the position was encumbered when he accepted the job, I later found out that Jones had willingly accepted the job because he was trying to escape from an ongoing investigation at his previous job. Similarly, the lady who had vacated the position before Dr. Jones had left hastily for another job assignment. Since this position was overseas, federal government personnel rules allowed her to maintain her "rights" to the job currently held by Jones upon her return from her overseas billet. Like

Dr. Jones, she had left to stave off disciplinary action against her for poor performance and disruptive workplace behavior. I would soon experience firsthand Betty Moore's poor leadership skills.

Her track record as a director mirrored that of Dr. Jones' toxic leadership style. Before me, her two most recent deputy directors had suffered under her conniving and manipulative ways. Before willingly taking a three-grade position downgrade from a GS-15 to a GS-12 to work at an Air Force installation in Japan, Moore had engaged in a profanity-laced tirade with one of her subordinates. The exchange between her and her female deputy had led to the police being called to de-escalate the situation. Sensing that the senior leadership team was contemplating taking adverse action against her, she quickly applied for and accepted a position in Japan with a substantial downgrade in position authority and responsibility so that she could avoid receiving any disciplinary action for her inappropriate behavior. Ironically, personnel rules stipulated that she could retain her GS-15 salary while in the lower grade overseas. Her subsequent male deputy in Japan would file an EEO complaint against her after suffering under her toxic leadership for over three years.

One day, I received an email asking the Director, EEO, to approve Ms. Moore's extension in Japan for another year. Although I was the acting Director of EEO, it was not my place to approve or disapprove this request. The deputy director of the agency, a senior executive service (SES) member who knew of Moore's prior transgressions, decided that things were going well in the EEO office and to leave her in Japan. The deputy sent an email to her that said, "Betty, your request for an additional one-year extension is approved." Knowing he would soon retire, a week passed, and the deputy changed his mind. He decided to "kick the can down the road" and not deal with Moore's antics. He sent her a second email saying, "Betty, this is about your recently approved extension for one year: it is now approved for two years." Upon receiving this notification, Moore was livid. She called the only remaining staff member during her tenure at the agency. All the former office personnel had left for other jobs. She had chased them all away. After taking her call, Nichole told me that Moore was irate. She had said to Nichole, "What is going on back there? That is my job!"

I could understand this response from Moore. Imagine if your company tells you, in essence, that you are not needed right now. Then imagine your boss following that up with, "We thought about it some more, and not only do we not need you, but we request you to stay away and never come back!" I realized at this point that there would be repercussions for me. I could imagine her trying to find out about me and asking, "Who was this guy leading an office where the senior leaders do not want me to come back?"

When the head of the agency found out about the deputy's plan to have her stay in Japan, she directed him to undo it. She argued that she had been in Japan long enough. Moore would either have to return to her position or give up her return rights. When informed of her new options, Betty came back. However, before she did, she tried to delay her return by arguing that her extension in Japan should remain in effect because she was selected to attend the Army's War College. The human capital directorate researched her claim and discovered this was not true. The agency director called one of her colleagues, a fellow lieutenant general in Japan, to request his assistance in directing Moore's return. Her War College claim would be the first of many lies she would tell throughout the next two years after arriving back at the agency.

When Moore finally returned to her position, she traveled constantly across the country, visiting the agency's geographically dispersed offices. Her justification for these trips was contrived. She could get away with this extensive travel because no one in the agency was overseeing her actions. Office staff members openly remarked about her travels being fraudulent, given that there was no business case for doing so with any return on investment for the agency. Some in the office contemplated filing an IG whistleblower complaint about her excessive air travel and hotel costs with the fraud, waste, and abuse hotline.

While traveling, she placed all responsibility on me for running the daily operations, including managing work products, directing the staff, and attending meetings in her place. Being out of the office and amassing extensive frequent flyer miles and Marriott Hotel rewards points is one thing; however, creating office strife by sending emails assigning "make-work" to staff members was demoralizing. The senior leaders knew that she was never in the office. It was almost as if they preferred it that way. It was as if they reasoned that the work was getting done, so why bother holding her accountable? The status quo meant they did not have to deal with her.

The agency director once held an "all-hands" meeting where she remarked, "Where is Betty? That's right; she is probably out of the office again." Those in attendance chuckled. After waiting a day or so, Moore caught wind of this and, upon her return, barged into my office and asked, "What happened at the all-hands meeting?" Knowing that one of her "moles" within the building had already told her, I feigned confusion. I asked her, "What do you mean what happened?" I went on, "The General recognized me by giving me one of Commander's Coins for when I acted as director before you returned to the agency. She then said something else, and those in attendance laughed." Betty became more livid and asked, "What did she say?" I responded, "I do not remember." I answered this way because she would have used my name to make a case against the General, saying, "Dr. Covert told me that you were making fun of me in an official setting…"

I once attended one of the Equal Employment Opportunity Commission's quarterly director's meetings in Moore's absence. She could not participate because she was out traveling on another one of her trips. Before the next session began, I told a colleague that I was looking for promotion opportunities and applying for GS-15 positions – someone a few rows away had overheard my conversation. This person blurted out, "You are looking for a job?" With a chuckle, he said, "That's going to interfere with Moore's travel plans!" It was apparent that she had openly bragged about what she was doing at our organization to fellow EEO practitioners across the federal government.

I would also have to attend her meetings at the agency. When she was in between trips, she would come out of her office to tell me to participate in a meeting she was required to attend, saying, "Tell them I am not here." When I refused, she said, "Okay, well, tell them I am with a customer then." Although my competence threatened Moore, she would still use me to attend her meetings with senior leaders out of fear of facing tough questions at the high-level meetings and without knowing the answers.

Apart from me, Moore did not supervise anyone on the staff. As her deputy, this was not uncommon. What was unusual was how she used me as her buffer to cause angst and strife with the other staff members daily. Her method was to divide and conquer. She would pit staff members against one another by spreading lies and falsehoods. Through me, she would assign work to them that was neither required to accomplish the mission nor added any value to the agency. "What kind of supervisor is Dr. Covert?" she would ask my subordinates behind my back. She posed this question to gather any derogatory information to use against me. In turn, my subordinates would inform me of what she was doing.

When I submitted a leave request for the time I had earned to go on a medical appointment or vacation, she would take no action to approve or disapprove it. On and on, this continued. She would intentionally "sit" on my leave requests and take no action on them to always keep me in the office.

In any situation, we always have choices. We can accept it, change it, or leave it. I left. I asked the deputy director to move me to another position within the agency once she made false allegations against me the day before Christmas. An investigation into her claims found them to be unsubstantiated. A part of me felt as though my leaving was a failure on my part. However, my rationale for doing so was after I came to terms with the fact the senior leadership team was unwilling to invest the time and energy to take any action against Moore despite the results from a recently completed climate survey, which under any other circumstances, would trigger a commander's inquiry or investigation. The substantial burden of serving as the buffer between her and the rest of the staff and her conniving and manipulative behaviors was untenable. I reached a point where I could no longer listen to her sing aloud, "I am dreaming of a white Christmas," whenever she was under duress or plotting another one of her schemes. Betty always defaulted to this weird coping mechanism. No matter the week or the month, her chiming out, "I am dreaming of a white Christmas," only added to the heavy cloud hanging over the office daily. All the while, I asked, "Why is this happening to me? What am I supposed to be learning from this?"

Leadership crucibles come in various shapes and forms. We are all put to the test at one point or another. How we react will be driven by who we are. Not knowing who we are before confronting a leadership crisis is a recipe for failure. While failure is the best teacher and part of learning and growing, our understanding of who we are is the best predictor of success during tumultuous change. Building our capacity to lead through the "fog of war" with flexibility and adaptability is paramount for employing the best leadership style for different settings.

News of my imminent departure left some staff members in tears while others exhibited fear, anger, and resentment towards me for leaving them behind. My measure of success was not reacting to her in ways that resulted in an adverse outcome, such as when the police had to respond to a verbal dispute between her and the previous person working in my position. If I were the problem, the leadership would not have moved me. In essence, they were saying that I was worth "saving." At the same time, the leadership team was, in essence, turning away from confronting the problem head-on.

Betty was an example of what Scott Gregory, in his article, *The Most Common Type of Incompetent Leader*, termed as an absentee leader. Worse than an incompetent boss is a leader in title only. Unlike Dr. Jones, whom many on the staff viewed as a ranting, narcissistic sociopath, Betty was psychologically detached from those she was supposed to lead. In hindsight, I have concluded that the senior leadership team chose to look the other way, as Betty was not overtly misbehaving. Without reason, such as when the police had to be called during her previous stint at the organization, she was now allowed to be a de facto leader – to come and go as she pleased without providing any leadership. On top of being manipulative, Betty avoided meaningful involvement with the team when she was in the office. She would find ways not to attend luncheons and to recognize office staff members before their departure to another job.

Betty had a good gig. She was allowed to enjoy the privileges and rewards of her leadership position without any accountability. She withdrew value from the organization without depositing any value back in. The cost of her absentee leadership was the destruction of office cohesion, productivity, and morale; it was the most stressful time in my career. More than what she did as a leader, it was what Betty did not do. My wife and I purchased a second Chihuahua during this time. Our first Chihuahua, "Brutus," had passed away four years carlier. I sought out our second Chihuahua, "Chester," to provide comfort and relief when away from my stressful work setting.

So why did Betty's bosses not do anything about the toxic environment she had created? I have asked myself this question numerous times. One answer is to avoid confrontation; they chose the easy wrong over the difficult right. Another explanation, which I believe to be the case, is that they had other leaders who required more time and energy. In our vast organization, other leaders caused more significant problems with even more overtly destructive behaviors.

Unlike her earlier transgression with the police having to be called, Betty's second stint with the agency did not reach a level of anything other than a low-priority problem. With other leaders across the agency accused of sexual harassment, fraud, and misuse of funds, we were left to fend for ourselves. Betty had learned from her past mistakes. She could fly under the radar of her leaders by not engaging in any acts that would make her a target. While they knew her shortcomings, the senior leaders had "bigger fish to fry." Betty's negative effect on the office was emotionally harming everyone.

Because all challenges are unique, there is no one-size-fits-all approach. How you will react will be based upon knowing who you are. It requires what Goleman identified as emotional intelligence: self-awareness, self-regulation, motivation, empathy, social skills, and adaptability. Knowing who we are allows us to overcome our crucibles while being comfortable in our skin – it requires perseverance and grit.

Emotional Intelligence (EI)

Influential leaders engage in an ongoing pursuit of self-awareness. Through self-reflection, we can build on what Daniel Goldman identified as our emotional intelligence. Instead of a set of definitive traits or characteristics, research shows that all successful leaders embody high self-awareness, self-regulation, motivation, empathy, and social skills. As leaders, we must first understand our own emotions while building the capacity to be sensitive to others' emotions. At the same time, we must manage our impulses based on our feelings as leaders. The components of EI are depicted in Figure 4 below. Each of these five traits consists of the skills that effective leaders exhibit apart from one's IQ score, amount of technical skill training, or formal education credentials. The point here is that all of us can strengthen our emotional intelligence on the journey to becoming high-performing leaders. While we each acquire different levels of emotional intelligence at birth, we can enhance our capacity in this area through practice.

The Five Components of Emotional Intelligence at Work

	Definition	Hallmarks
Self-awareness	• The ability to recognize and understand your moods, emotions, and drives as well as their effect on others.	• Self-confidence • Realistic self-assessment • A self-deprecating sense of humor
Self-Regulation	• The ability to control or redirect disruptive impulses and moods. • The propensity to suspend judgment - to think before acing.	• Trustworthiness and integrity • Comfort with ambiguity • Openness to change
Motivation	• A passion to work for reasons that go beyond money or status. • A propensity to pursue goals with energy and persistence.	• Strong drive to achieve • Optimism, even in the face of failure • Organizational commitment
Empathy	• The ability to understand the emotional makeup of other people. • Skill in treating people according to their emotional reactions.	• Expertise in building and retaining talent • Cross-cultural sensitivity • Service to clients and customers
Social Skill	• Proficiency in managing relationships and building networks. • An ability to find common ground and build rapport.	• Effectiveness in leading change • Persuasiveness • Expertise in building and leading teams

Figure 4

Source: Harvard Business Review

"Self-awareness is the ability to take an honest look at your life without any attachment to it being right or wrong, good or bad."

- Debbie Ford

Self-awareness

Goldman defines self-awareness as knowing one's strengths and weaknesses. This component of EI also includes personal initiative and optimism. It is the skill of understanding what drives us, knowing our values, and being aware of our impact on others. Self-awareness also involves understanding your emotions and needs and their effect on work relationships. The hallmarks of self-awareness include self-confidence, realistic self-assessment, and a self-deprecating sense of humor. This component of EI is paramount for building the second element of emotional intelligence, self-regulation.

In her article, *What Self-Awareness Really Is (and How to Cultivate it),* Tasha Eurich posits two types of self-awareness. Eurich labels the first category as *internal self-awareness.* This type of awareness represents how well we see our thoughts, feelings, values, passions, and aspirations and how they fit with our environment. Internal self-awareness includes additional factors such as understanding how we impact others.

The second category, *external self-awareness*, refers to understanding how others view us with the above factors. Eurich's research shows that when leaders see themselves as their followers do, they are more likely to be adept at displaying empathy and considering others' points of view.

Seeing ourselves more clearly leads to more confidence. Leaders' heightened internal and external self-awareness results in more decisive decision-making. Self-awareness also promotes more effective communication, which leads to more effective leaders and more satisfied employees.

"The first and best victory is to conquer self."

- Plato

Self-regulation

Goldman defines self-regulation as controlling or redirecting disruptive impulses and moods. This EI component also includes the propensity to suspend judgment – to think before acting. This capacity is akin to the Roman poet Horace's warning, "Rule your mind, or it will rule you."

The hallmarks of self-regulation include trustworthiness and integrity, comfort with ambiguity, and openness to change. Below, I provide an example of a colleague who once exhibited behaviors inconsistent with self-regulation – thinking of potential consequences before acting on his impulses.

In the story above, my emotions toward Betty were contempt and frustration - contempt for not showing any commitment or accountability and frustration for not showing any intention to change. My self-awareness allowed me to recognize my emotions, and my self-regulation allowed me to control my feelings – to think before acting impulsively for my leadership challenge. Below, I provide an example where self-regulation is absent. This scenario also shows the potential pitfalls when we do not build our emotional intelligence, including the ability to build upon self-regulation.

I once sent an email to all the organization's senior leaders. In the message, I said, "Please ensure all of your assigned personnel have completed the mandatory equal opportunity training by the end of the fiscal year. Thanks." Many of those on the addressee replied with a short "Okay" or "Got it, thanks," while others did not respond. This non-response from most was acceptable, given that my message did not solicit one, only a requested action. One staff member sent me a much different reply than the rest.

Mike, an Army Lieutenant Colonel in charge of the installation's military police unit, said, "Quit sending me your sh!t." I replied to his email and asked, "Don't you have bullets on your OER to demonstrate support of EEO?" The "bullets" I referred to were short statements on his officer evaluation report or "OER." Immediately after receipt of my email, Mike, referring to his 9 MM service weapon, responded, "I have sixteen bullets, fifteen in the clip and one in the chamber. How many do you want me to send your way?" I responded to him by stating, "I see you are communicating a threat through a government computer." With this email from me, the military policeman's emails ceased abruptly.

Before this exchange, Mike and I were peers and colleagues. We sat next to each other in staff meetings and often joked with one another. On some days, when patrolling in his military truck on the installation, he would pull up behind me and turn on his lights and sirens. When I started to pull over, he would drive by with a smirk as he gave me "the finger."

As a jokester who went up to and sometimes over the line, Mike regarded me as someone comfortable enough to carry out his shenanigans. However, he was unsure if he had overstepped on the day of our email exchange. This episode introduces the importance of self-control and regulation. Self-regulation is the act or condition of regulating oneself from within instead of through other external sources, such as friends, co-workers, or a boss. While I did not take offense to his actions, Mike's shenanigans exhibited a lack of self-regulation in a professional setting.

This story could have had a very different outcome for Mike. As leaders, we must be able to modulate our feelings to include our actions and reactions. Without this internal discipline, we run the risk of external forces directing our paths with undesirable results.

Motivation

Goldman defines motivation as a trait common in all effective leaders. Leaders with high motivation and EI achieve to achieve. That is, instead of being driven by external factors, such as money or prestigious job titles, individuals with the potential to excel at leadership are those driven to succeed – they are motivated to achieve. An extraordinary passion most commonly demonstrates the motivation trait for a job, goal, objective, or mission. The hallmarks of motivation include a strong drive to achieve, optimism, even in the face of failure, and organizational commitment. Leaders with this trait are passionate about their work and love to learn new things.

High-motivation people can maintain optimism even when confronted with daunting challenges or setbacks. Highly motivated leaders are adept at combining self-regulation with achievement motivation to remain resilient. Finally, high motivation EI is when leaders commit to the organization and those they lead.

One measure of gauging whether or not you are an effective leader begins with answering if you are self-motivated. Personal motivation embodies the type of leader you would follow. Only then can you motivate others to achieve your goals and the goals of those you lead.

"As a leader, you should always start with where people are before you try to take them where you want them to go."

- Jim Rohn

Empathy

Empathy is associated with moving from self-awareness to awareness and acceptance of the importance and validity of others' emotions. Goldman defines empathy as a leader's ability to consider employees' feelings when making decisions. The hallmarks of empathy include expertise in building and retaining talent, cross-cultural sensitivity, and service to clients and customers.

Empathy EI is often confused with leaders trying to please everyone within their sphere of influence. In the context of Goldman's EI, empathy is about leaders having the ability to understand individuals' and team members' emotional makeup to facilitate the completion of the mission. One aspect of empathy is taking the time to listen to and understand others' feelings. Another aspect is that leaders use this understanding to move those they lead and the organization forward to reach successful outcomes. Closely aligned with empathy is the social skills trait.

Social Skills

Goleman defines social skills as managing relationships and building networks proficiently. This component of EI includes individuals who can find common ground while building a rapport. The hallmarks of high social skills include effectiveness in leading change, persuasiveness, and expertise in building and leading teams. This intelligence is precious for leaders working with diverse individuals and organizations.

Understanding, building, and applying our EI to leadership challenges can foster successful outcomes. While these "crucibles" can be emotionally and physically taxing, these tests are also opportunities to gauge where we stand in each area of EI. In turn, we learn more about ourselves – our strengths and weaknesses.

In Chapter 10, our discussion turns to what our leadership legacies will be. Before moving on to the next section, take a moment to answer the questions in the below exercise.

What is your leadership crucible? Explain.

____

____

____

____

How did the leadership crisis change who you are now? Explain.

____

____

____

____

What did you learn from your leadership test?

____

____

____

What would you do differently?

Give an example where you applied Emotional Intelligence (EI) to a leadership challenge. What was the outcome?

Give an example where you missed an opportunity to apply EI to a leadership challenge. What was the outcome? What could you have done differently? What did you learn?

____

____

____

____

Which component(s) of EI do you view as a personal strength? Why?

____

____

____

____

Which component(s) of EI do you view as areas for improvement? Why?

____

____

____

CHAPTER 10

The Night The Helicopters Crashed: Your Leadership Legacy

No single factor is rarely the cause of a catastrophic event, accident, or leadership failure. An incident analysis often reveals a chain of events leading to the catastrophe. Adverse factors and the compounding of errors set the crash on its tragic course. Rarely are such events a perfect storm not to be preventable. More times than not, multiple leadership failures exist. So, too, was the case when two Army Sikorsky UH-60 Black Hawk helicopters crashed.

The battalion commander told his subordinate pilots, leading up to the crash, "No more dropping the loads." An aviation brigade and its corresponding battalions aim to fly tactical missions supporting the division's assets, including personnel and equipment. The standard operating procedure (SOP) for a helicopter losing speed, altitude, or visual contact with the ground is to drop the load, regain altitude, hover, and contact the local airport tower's air traffic control (ATC) for further instructions. The "load" can range from a pallet of supplies, artillery equipment, or military vehicles such as the High Mobility Multipurpose Wheeled Vehicle (HMMWV), more commonly referred to as a Humvee. Dropping "the load" can be expensive and curtail the successful completion of the mission. The battalion commander's blanket order to not drop loads went against the SOP. Rather than prioritizing safety, the commander focused on his performance evaluation.

Many of the helicopters in the Army inventory are in recognition of Native American leaders and tribes. The Black Hawk pays tribute to the war chief and leader of the Sauk tribe. No matter the type of helicopter, crashes in an Army aviation brigade are never a recipe for leaders receiving their next promotion.

Before the previous brigade commander's tenure ended, he ordered the cessation of all flying 90 days before his scheduled change of command. Military training missions are inherently dangerous; training to prepare to fight and win our Nation's war requires it. The prior brigade commander's order to stop flying before he left is another example of leaders concerned more about their future assignments and potential promotion to the General Officer Corps than preparing their brigade to "train as you fight." Both are examples of leaders putting their interests ahead of choosing the hard right over the easy wrong.

In the early morning of the next day after the crash, the brigade senior leader team assembled as a crisis management team at the headquarters building. The team consisted of the commanders and command sergeants majors (CSMs) of the three aviation battalions, along with key staff from the brigade, including the aviation brigade's senior safety officer, the brigade commander, and his executive officer and command sergeant major. With everyone assembled, the brigade commander entered the conference room to begin the meeting and implement the crisis plan. One aviation battalion CSM yelled, "Where is Sergeant Major Whittingham?" He was referring to the brigade commander's command sergeant major. Another battalion sergeant major flippantly remarked, "Why don't you try calling Sergeant Smith's house." Sergeant Smith was not the brigade's sergeant major's wife. She was a subordinate enlisted Soldier assigned to one of the brigade's support companies.

My wife and I attended the musical "RENT" downtown a month earlier. We were in seats up front near the orchestra section. When the musical ended, I stood and turned around to watch the audience exiting as the auditorium lights came on. I locked eyes with someone I knew sitting in the first row of the upper balcony. It was CSM Whittingham. Sitting next to him was Sergeant Smith. I held my gaze; I wanted him to know I saw what he was doing – fraternizing with a subordinate Soldier in his brigade as a married man. Inside the conference room in the early morning hours after the helicopter crash, someone from the brigade called Sergeant Smith's government-furnished housing; CSM Wittingham answered the phone. He was somewhere he was not supposed to be.

In Army basic training, the drill sergeants drove into us recruits' heads that when we were on the M-16 firing range, anyone could yell out "cease-fire!" if they were witnessing an unsafe act. The same held for the night of the helicopter crash; anyone could and should speak up if something dangerous was in the process of happening. The aviation brigade's senior safety officer, a Chief Warrant Officer (CWO) – 04, did. Unforcasted heavy fog and rain were now severely reducing visibility. The battalion commander overrode his safety officer's concerns; he instructed the mission to continue by modifying the flight plan. Instead of proceeding to the planned landing zone (LZ

1), the Black Hawks would now divert to LZ 2. This modification and the chain of events up until this point set in motion what would happen next.

On the night of the incident, the weather deteriorated halfway into the mission. With the brigade commander overseeing the mission from a prop plane, he listened in as the warrant officer voiced his alarm over the radio. The battalion commander ordered the mission to continue with an altered LZ. The brigade commander did not intervene; the senior commander erred on the side of "letting his subordinate commander command."

The five Black Hawks, flying single file to LZ 1, were now directed to divert to LZ 2. Making a 120-degree turn to the new LZ, the lead helicopter eventually lost visual contact with the ground. Instead of stopping to hover, the pilot decided to continue to LZ 2. At the same time, the trailing helicopter was losing speed and altitude. The pilot decided to race to LZ 2 by deviating from the prescribed flight path by turning right, hoping to make it to the new LZ and not dropping the load. The lead and trailing helicopters met at the LZ at the same time. They struck one another head-on, pitched upward, and then both fell to the ground, killing all passengers except for the lead Black Hawk pilot. The passengers were each aircraft's co-pilot, crew chiefs, and infantrymen supporting the training mission.

When the investigation team arrived from the Aviation Center in Alabama, formerly named Fort Rucker, they took over the brigade's conference as their operations center. After interviewing key leaders and reviewing the data and wreckage, the investigative team focused on the human factors that led to the mishap. As the brigade's equal opportunity advisor (EOA), who reported directly to CSM Whittingham and the brigade commander, I handed over the requested command climate surveys for the brigade's units to the investigators. The surveys revealed a toxic command climate for the battalion whose helicopters crashed.

What if the brigade commander had intervened and told the battalion commander to abort the mission due to the worsening weather conditions? Did the safety officer protest vehemently enough? Why didn't the lead pilot follow the SOP, which required him to stop, hover, and contact the ATC when he lost visual contact with the ground? Why did the trailing pilot not drop the Humvee when losing speed and altitude? How did the command climate affect his decision to disregard proper procedures and deviate from the flight path while hastily trying to get to the second LZ? If the trailing pilot had followed standard procedures, he would have suffered the wrath of his commander for disobeying his order not to drop the load, but he and all of the Soldiers who perished would still be alive! However, no single cause led to the tragic outcome; it was multiple factors, as is often the case.

I, too, became part of the investigation. The investigator did not ask me about the climate surveys, which were my responsibility to administer, analyze, and make final reports with recommendations. Instead, he asked me about CSM Whittingham; I remember asking myself, "What does the sergeant's major sleeping with a subordinate enlisted Soldier have to do with two helicopters crashing? The investigator's demeanor towards me was adversarial. Point blank, he asked, "Why did you not say anything about Sergeant Major

Whittingham? I replied, "I did. I went directly to him and told him that a lot of Soldiers had come to me making snide remarks about him sleeping with Sergeant Smith. I told him I was not saying he did or didn't; if he did, it was probably a good idea for him to stop. I left his office, immediately went into the XO's office, and told him verbatim what I told the sergeant major." Then, the investigator closed his notepad and left my office.

The sergeant major was my first-line supervisor, who wrote my performance appraisal. I could have put my head in the sand and chose not to confront him. However, you never know what subsequent events could bring your character and integrity into question. Knowing who you are provides the foundation and roadmap to do what is right in confronting challenging situations.

To be sure, all of us can learn leadership, and poor leadership can be unlearned. It requires a willingness to change. Change occurs through an honest assessment of self. Knowing your strengths and weaknesses and becoming more self-aware can help you build on the leadership tenets in this book. The practice of leadership never ends; when you think you have mastered it, prepare to fail. Hopefully, you can learn from your failures before a catastrophic event. In the end, your leadership is your legacy.

"Achievement comes to people who are able to do great things for themselves. Success comes when they lead followers to do great things for them. But, a legacy is created only when leaders put their people in a position to do great things without them. The legacy of successful leaders lives on through the people they touch along the way."

\- John Maxwell

Legacy

In 1998, I penned my obituary. I did so as part of a class assignment while working on my doctorate in educational leadership at the University of Southern California. Professor Bill Tierney, who would later become my dissertation advisor, included this requirement in his advanced qualitative methods course. As I recall it, my focus at the time was on completing this assignment so I could move on to finishing the remainder of the course readings and the final twenty-page paper. I also remember that most of what I had written was goals I had hoped to achieve in my lifetime.

I forgot about this until I penned my obituary a second time in 2017. This time, I did so as part of a class assignment while participating in Harvard University's Senior Executive Fellows Program. My second obituary was different. While it listed past accomplishments and things I hoped to achieve, it included something more critical. This time, my draft obituary covered how I had made a difference in the lives of others. Once the exercise was complete, the professor suggested, "In the end, no one will care where you went to school. No one will remember your job titles or how much money you made. Your legacy will be how you made a difference in someone else's life."

I left Harvard thinking more about this. I found myself questioning what impact I have had on others. While driving away from Cambridge, Massachusetts, back to Virginia, I thought about when I left home for the first time at seventeen to enter Army basic training at Fort Jackson, South Carolina. In 1983, four days after high school graduation, I flew out of Buffalo, New York – my first time flying. A few hours later, I landed in Columbia, South Carolina, and met the man who would be my drill sergeant, Drill Sergeant Marshall. Many say that you never forget your drill sergeant's name. I can attest this to be true. I still remember Drill Sergeant Marshall and what he said to me.

Halfway through basic training, Drill Sergeant Marshall pulled all of us trainees aside to counsel us individually on our performance. I remember it was my first time speaking to him when I was not standing at attention or a modified version of the same, known as parade rest. I also remember it was the first time I saw him speaking calmly and sharing some personal information about himself with me. I, too, became relaxed. He asked me a question at some point, and I responded with, "Yeah." As soon as I mouthed this response, I realized my mistake as he turned, glared at me with reddening eyes, and said, "Yeah? Oh, so I am your f*!*ing buddy now or something?" Before he could finish, I shouted, "No, Drill Sergeant!" I remember this exchange to this day. My lesson is to remember that you are always "on" and never to let your guard down. However, what Drill

Sergeant Marshall said at the end of our counseling session impacted me more. He said, "Covert, you are going to go far."

I have thought a lot about his remark over the years. Now, maybe Drill Sergeant Marshall said this to every recruit. Perhaps he told it to only a select few. What mattered was that Marshall said it to me. He made a difference in this seventeen-year-old's life, even though he would never have known this. As a leader, Drill Sergeant Marshall was someone I watched every day for twelve weeks in the summer of 1983. Because he was someone I respected for his commitment and competence, his words mattered to me and served to motivate and push me forward in my military career.

Years later, as a mid-career staff sergeant, I was counseling one of my Soldiers in Germany. I remember telling Specialist Jenkins that he should consider applying for "Green to Gold," a program for enlisted Soldiers to gain their bachelor's degree and become commissioned officers. I did not say this to all the Soldiers in my platoon. I did not say it to a select few. I told Specialist Jenkins about it only because I saw his potential. I was not sure if he saw the same thing in himself. I thought no more about this conversation until twenty years later when Specialist Jenkins, now LTC Jenkins, contacted me out of nowhere. When I asked him how he was doing and what he was up to, he said he was getting ready to retire as a Lieutenant Colonel. He asked me, "Do you remember what you told me about becoming a commissioned officer in Germany? Well, I listened to what you said; thank you!" I believe I made a difference in his life.

While writing this book, I reached out to former employees whom I have had the privilege to lead and asked them to write about what they had learned from me. While I had remained in contact with them occasionally, over five years had passed since we had last worked together. One EEO specialist, now working with the Department of the Air Force, replied,

Dr. Covert was tough but fair. He was very decisive when making a decision. His leadership style was distinct, with a quality that made the work environment productive and met the objective. When I say he was tough but fair, he set the standards, followed them, and worked alongside us to accomplish the mission. Another excellent quality I admired about Dr. Covert's leadership was his ability to continually provide purpose, direction, and motivation even though we were understaffed. He was a great communicator and always kept us informed. One tradition he maintained was celebrating our birthdays. He made that his thing. On our birthday, he would take us wherever we wanted to go for lunch and pay for our meals. Not only that, he treated the entire staff to dessert! This act was impressive and went a long way with me; not only was this a kind gesture, but it was a good team builder as well. Dr. Covert was mainly serious but also had a sense of humor.

Most importantly, Dr. Covert set me up for success. As a newbie in the civilian workforce, he ensured we all received various training for our professional development. The unique thing was he was looking out for our future. He always said, "Don't let this be your stopping place," he meant that. He provided the tools for us to compete with everyone else. Dr. Covert has moved up the chain in life but hasn't forgotten where he came from. I continue to reach out to him and even trust him to mentor my son!

Another former employee now working with the Department of the Navy in Norfolk, Virginia, replied by saying,

I learned to study my craft and know what I am talking about. I saw your candidness as a leader and realized that you must be confident when dealing with your employees. You didn't "sugarcoat" anything with us. We knew what you expected as a leader. I learned that education is an ongoing process by watching your continuous growth, even at your level. You showed me that it is okay to take care of the staff and do things that might help morale and correct or discipline when someone displays unacceptable behavior. You showed me that I shouldn't get comfortable with where I am if I expect to grow; that means maybe having to move into other positions outside my comfort zone not to become stagnant.

A previous employee, presently at the Department of Homeland Security, said,

I learned always to do the right thing to protect my credibility and reputation. You showed me how a leader controls their emotions and impulses under duress. Finally, I learned from you that you must teach, mentor, and guide your employees but never be afraid to correct or discipline them. You have to offer continuous feedback and correct issues as soon as they occur; you're not there to be your employee's friend.

All of the above responses touch on many of the factors of leadership covered in this book. As Peter Drucker makes clear,

"…effective leadership is to earn trust. Otherwise, there won't be any followers – and the only definition of a leader is someone with followers. To trust a leader, it is not necessary to like him. Nor is it necessary to agree with him. Trust is the conviction that the leader means what he says. It is a belief in something very old-fashioned called integrity." Drucker emphasizes, "A leader's actions and a leader's professed beliefs must be congruent, or at least compatible. Effective leadership is based primarily on being consistent."

While writing this chapter, I also thought about the question Dr. Jones had posed years earlier when he asked, "Tell me what your former supervisors would say about you?" In turn, I reached out to some of my former bosses and asked them to write about what type of leader I was. A retired Air Force colonel and now civilian executive director at an air base wing said,

Clint never let an issue get him emotionally unbalanced, no matter how hard, ridiculous, or frustrating. His calm, cool approach to anything was balanced by thoughtfulness and engaged interest in the person, not just the issue. Clint is knowledgeable; he knows his business and responsibilities better than anyone around him.

The same holds for your leadership legacy. While reading your obituary, no one will fixate on how high you ascended in your professional career. However, people will remember if you had a positive impact on them. While you may never know the impact you have left behind, you will have left your leadership imprint just the same. The question guiding our assessment of ourselves is an internal examination of who we have helped in the past, who we are helping now, and who we will help in the future. The answers give us our purpose. How we do it defines our passion. The results of our impact on others are our legacies.

Who are you? In the preface of this book, I suggest that asking this question helps us better understand who we have been, who we are now, and who we aspire to be. Why should I care? This question is designed to answer, "Is who I am now someone others would willingly follow? If not, why?" My goal in writing this book was to look at leadership through a different lens, to direct your path in finding your way to becoming the leader you aspire to be. On your last day on earth, will the leader you became be the leader you could have become? What will be your legacy? To get to these answers, we must first self-reflect on where we have been. Acknowledging our past gives us an understanding of where we are now and where we are going – to get to where we want to be.

Yes, we are who we are. However, we can shape who we are and change things about ourselves. Doing so requires hard work. It forces us to break away from some of our habits and leave our comfort zone. It is this personal discomfort that leads to growth. Growth occurs when we confront new things and learn from them. Likewise, some of the best learning takes place through experiencing failure. As Bill George noted, pushing past our crucibles, weaknesses, and setbacks allows us to refine our authentic selves further. In turn, we become more authentic leaders. Part of building our authenticity is the ability to persist in overcoming obstacles in our leadership journey.

"Thankfully, perseverance is a good substitute for talent."

\- Steve Martin

Perseverance

Perseverance is a continued effort to do or achieve something despite obstacles, difficulties, failure, or opposition – a steadfastness for mastering or completing a skill. As the Carthaginian General Hannibal remarked, "We will either find a way or make one." This demonstration of steadfastness and the ability to persist is an invaluable leadership trait. Perseverance is also a commitment to always learning new things.

While working on my doctorate, the faculty would always impress upon my cohort the importance of finishing the dissertation. Everyone in academic circles understands that conferring a doctorate signifies the completion of a terminal degree and represents the ability to conduct scholarly research on a particular topic independently. More so, it means the ability to persist. Writing is hard, even for academics. The same holds for leaders. While leadership can be learned, its successful application requires trial and error and steadfastness - it is not easy and requires perseverance.

In her book Grit: The Power of Passion and Perseverance, Angela Duckworth suggests that the best predictor of success is "grit." Other factors, such as IQ or natural talent, have limitations in predicting who does and does not succeed. As Duckworth states, "Our potential is one thing. What we do with it is quite another."

Therefore, we cannot honestly know or reach our full potential without first tapping into it. Whether writing a book, running a marathon, or becoming a better leader, all these endeavors are hard. Regardless of the challenge, we can harness our innate gifts and persevere to reach our goals. Perseverance is an act of being comfortable while being uncomfortable.

The same holds for your leadership legacy. The most critical factors for confronting and overcoming your leadership crucibles are your leadership passion and perseverance. Your grit is just as important as your ability to practice self-control and delay short-term gratification.

What is the most challenging physical activity that you have ever completed? Do you remember that feeling of physical and mental exertion? For me, it was running the Miami Marathon in 2016. Two years earlier, I had run the half marathon course there. I started near the American Airlines Arena in downtown Miami and ran across the Macarthur Causeway into South Beach, jogging along Ocean Drive. At mile marker five, I thought about an earlier conversation with my father about running my first half marathon. When I told him about this on the phone, he asked, "Mark, why would you want to do that?" To this day, my parents still refer to me by my middle name. My dad was concerned about me taking on such a grueling challenge at age 49. I told my father about my earlier experience with the Navy SEALs. Running had become a way to train my mind to *become comfortable with being uncomfortable.* Our conversation ended with me assuring my father that I had prepared adequately for this undertaking and that everything would be okay. Before hanging up, I remember telling him, "And besides, Dad, after the first five miles, they are all uncomfortable!"

I finished my first half marathon that day in two hours and 35 minutes. Two years later, I was set to run my first full marathon. Having run there before, I chose Miami because I was familiar with the first portion of the course. Two critical thoughts were racing through my mind that day. These feelings are something I will never forget. The first happened at mile marker 13 and the second at mile marker 22. Near the halfway point, I wanted to quit. Near the end of the race, I was overtaken by a strong desire, not wanting to stop for fear of what would happen if I did!

My wife and I had planned to spend a few days vacationing in South Beach after my run. We reasoned that a few days of rest would be warranted, not only to celebrate my triumph but also for me to recuperate enough for the long drive back to Virginia. However, last-minute work commitments prevented my wife from accompanying me on the trip. We adjusted our plan. Now, she would fly down the night before my run. On the marathon day, I stood in a crowd of over 39,000 runners without my most stalwart supporter. A winter storm had blanketed the northeast, shutting down all airport travel. Now, I would run my first marathon without my wife waiting at the finish line. Marian would have to resort to watching my progress at home with a tracking application on television.

Later, she told me how she watched as a blip on the screen showed my progress along the route. As I moved along the course, the blip would advance on the screen as I crossed each mile marker. At mile marker 19, the screen went blank. My wife told me later, "A part of me knew everything was all right, and this was just a glitch in the tracker. I knew you were going to make it. But there was another part of me that was worried. I was so glad you called and said you had done it!"

Back at mile marker 13 that day, I wanted to pack it in and call it a day. As I prepared to turn right off Flagler Street and head toward SE 2nd Street, I neared the half-marathon breakaway point. If I turned left, I would be close to the finish line for the half-marathon course. If I turned right, I would head southwest, out of downtown Miami, to complete the remaining 13.1 miles for the full marathon. Thoughts in my mind told me to turn left and call it a day. My body was aching, and I felt there was no way I could turn right and head out of town to run another 13.1 miles. I remember thinking Marian would understand when I told her I did not have it in me that day. I remember looking at other runners with full marathon-colored bibs making the turn to stop at the half marathon. I remember rationalizing that I would not be the only one registered for the full marathon who chose to stop and complete only the half marathon. I was now coming up on the orange warning cones dividing the street to direct the runners on their appropriate path at the breakaway point.

I had to make a choice. I remember reasoning that those close to me would understand if I stopped. After all, it was my first attempt. As I crept closer to justify in my mind a rational explanation for quitting, my flight-or-fight response was to turn right and proceed southwest and complete the remainder of the full marathon. The sounds of impatient motorists honking as the police held them up to allow us runners to pass were replaced by sounds of celebration. The noise from the music and cheering crowds faded as I headed out of town toward mile marker 14. Now, on the outskirts of downtown Miami, I ran parallel to Little Havana and then toward Coconut Grove. People often ask, "What do you think about while you run?" I respond by saying, "For me, I reach a point where all I am thinking about is putting one foot in front of the other."

I will never forget this – the feeling of having to choose under duress. That day, I was at a fork in the road – I had to decide on a way forward. The choice was more challenging to make mentally than physically. At mile marker 22, it was more physical than mental. At the halfway point, I had to wrestle in my mind with the desire to stop. At mile marker 22, I was fighting with the opposite feeling – not wanting to quit. At this point, I felt physical stress in my body that I had never felt before. I could sense that if I stopped to walk, my body would lock up, and I would not be able to finish. This feeling is also something I will never forget – by *becoming comfortable with being uncomfortable*, I was able to make good choices, complete the run, and realize my goal. To persevere also requires the willingness to adapt.

Change: Adapt or Die

When it comes to change, Peter Senge suggests, "People don't resist change. They resist being changed!" Senge's observation points out that change must come from within – we must be willing to adapt. One required reading from a professional development school I attended was an article written by then Brigadier General David A. Fastabend and Robert H. Simpson. The paper "Adapt or Die: The Imperative for a Culture of Innovation in the United States Army" called for building a culture of innovation within the U.S. Army to match the rapid pace of change across the globe. The crux of their argument was that continuous adaptation is critical to institutional survival for our armed forces.

The same holds for us as individual leaders – we must be able to adapt to remain relevant. As Robert E. Quinn points out, "One key to successful leadership is continuous personal change. Personal Change is a reflection of our inner growth and empowerment." Just as the military confronts an ever-changing battlefield, we as leaders operate within a fluid work environment surrounded by change. If we cannot adjust to our changing surroundings, we become ineffective; in essence, we either adapt or die.

In the final section of this book, I provide some concluding thoughts. Everyone will have different takeaways from reading this book. My overarching goal is to cement in your mind the lessons you have learned on your way to becoming a better leader. Before moving on to this book's final part, answer the questions in the below exercise.

<u>**EXERCISE**</u>

What is your story?

How is your story created? How is your story told? Who are the authors of your story?

How does your story influence your actions and your relationships with others?

How has your understanding of who you are impacted your ability to lead yourself and others?

Has who you are been shaped by considerations about what your leadership legacy will be? How? Why?

How does your story influence your leadership?

Describe a time when you embraced change.

Describe a time when you were resistant to change.

Have you ever penned your obituary? If so, what did it say? Why?

____

____

____

____

If you have not, take a moment and write your obituary.

____

____

____

____

How did writing your obituary make you feel? Explain.

____

____

____

____

"Watch your thoughts; they become your words. Watch your words; they become your actions. Watch your actions; they become your habits. Watch your habits; they become your character. Watch your character; it becomes your destiny."

— Anonymous

CONCLUSION

Yes, everyone has a story to tell. As you are near the end of this book, I hope that the time you invested in reading my story has translated into an opportunity for you to learn more about yourself. If my story has in some way inspired you to further excel in your life journey and pursuits, then I have succeeded. Part of this growth will be the changes you make moving forward. For some, minor tweaks or adjustments may be all that is needed. For others, the change will include significant course corrections. That is okay. It is how we grow. When we stop growing, we begin to die.

At the beginning of this book, I lamented about too many stories going untold. I challenge you to tell your story. As I mentioned, our stories inform others who we are. Telling your story is an opportunity for personal growth and motivation for those you lead. Reflecting on your story will inspire and push you forward in your life's journey and pursuits.

One of the outgrowths of our life stories is fresh perspectives or new ways of thinking about a leadership challenge or problem. Moving forward, the trials and tribulations you will experience will serve either as an affirmation of your current life path or as a stimulus to make a change. Just as important is telling your story; it will give you more authenticity when others decide whether to follow you as their leader.

Who am I? I hope that you now have a deep understanding of who you are. I also hope you understand why others will care enough to want to follow you as their leader. If so, your story will resonate with those you lead. From the outset, this book's premise was that while the what, when, where, how, and why elements of leadership are interconnected, the *"who"* aspect drives how we respond in our interactions with others. If my story served as a credible segue for you, the reader, to introduce the different concepts of leadership covered in this book, then I have succeeded.

Yes, to a large extent, we are who we are. However, given that you are still reading this book, I believe you did not fall prey to reaching a foregone conclusion that individuals cannot change. I also hope you have found it helpful to answer the question, "Who am I?" Like me, who you are is something that does not remain static. Upon reflection, we all have an "Ah-ha!" moment when we realize that our good and bad choices, successes and failures, and other lived experiences make us who we are today. As we proceed, we also come closer to becoming who we are supposed to be in leading ourselves and others.

While reading this book and completing the exercises at the end of each chapter, I hope you also engaged in multiple conversations with yourself about leadership. Reflecting on what makes good and bad leaders will direct your path to being the leader you aspire to be. Getting the most out of this book required you to engage in self-reflection throughout each chapter. It also needed you to be truly honest with yourself. For some of you, I am sure this was not easy. I applaud those of you who used this opportunity to dig deep, revisiting things from your past that you had forgotten about or wished not to bring back to the surface. The resurfacing of the feelings attached to your fears, past slights, failures, and regrets was the first step in overcoming the impediments to your personal growth and becoming a better leader.

These questions served as your starting point to further explore the emotions that surfaced during moments of quiet reflection. Identifying the root cause of these feelings has led you to own the lessons you have learned from these experiences, including understanding what you can do differently moving forward. Like me, you have experienced success and suffered setbacks and failures.

Whether in our personal or professional lives, we either have or will experience adversity. For those who have not skipped to the back of this book, the following epilogue reemphasizes that it is never a question of "if," only a question of "when" we will have to face the next storm. How you react to these leadership crises will be determined primarily by knowing who you are. All the while, someone will be watching you. You will be defined as a leader not by what you say but by what you do – your words must match your actions. Also, your words on Monday must be the same on Tuesday, Wednesday, Thursday, etc. People appreciate consistency from their leaders. This consistency builds trust as people come to know and understand their leaders' standard practices, behaviors, and expectations.

My goal in telling my story herein is to connect to the tenets in this book, such as the importance of humility. One premise is that learning about ourselves must acknowledge how our past, beginning in early childhood, shaped who we are today. While reading this book, if you were able to resist merely glossing over or not taking the time to reflect on how your past mistakes have shaped who you are at this present moment, I believe you have gained tremendous personal growth. I also think you are humbler for doing so.

From the outset, I intended to write a book about leadership from a new perspective. I also desired this to be a book about hope. As you near the end, I hope you can say aloud, "I know who I am, or at least who I want to be." From here forward, the question becomes, how will you apply what you have learned about yourself to get to where you want to be?

<u>EXERCISE</u>

What did you learn about yourself by reading this book?

____

____

____

____

Moving forward, how will you apply what you have learned?

____

____

____

____

What parts of leadership do you want to learn more about?

____

____

____

What courses of action will you take to grow personally and professionally?

Have you told your story yet? If not, why?

EPILOGUE

While writing this book, I experienced having to get a 10-millimeter kidney stone dislodged from my urinary tract. The stone was too large to pass on its own. Anyone who has felt the pain of kidney stones can testify to the aggravating pain accompanying it. Some have compared the pain to a woman going through childbirth. My experience started in the morning with stomach pains that slowly increased in intensity. My wife had already left in a separate car for Hampton, Virginia. We planned to spend the next few days there with her family on Christmas. I began the hour-and-a-half drive to my mother-in-law's house at around eleven that morning.

About thirty minutes into the drive on I-64 East, I experienced highly intense, sharp pains in my abdomen and lower back. At this point, I immediately knew what was happening. I did not care what the passengers in the vehicles next to me thought as I was driving and grunting out loud. The grimace on my face and my movements while trying to reposition myself in the seat as if to transfer the pain must have been something to behold. I recalled seeing my dad doing the same thing years ago as a kid as he drove to the hospital for a kidney stone he was trying to pass. The memory had stuck in my mind because it was the first time I had seen what I thought was my dad crying. Now, I was the one with my eyes watering in kidney-stone pain.

I did not pull off the highway. I knew that I had to get to the hospital. I reasoned that pulling over would only prolong getting there. When I arrived at the outskirts of Hampton, I took exit 261 to proceed towards the hospital. I called Marian once I arrived in the parking lot. Shortly after that, the diagnosis was a kidney stone. The only urologist on call that day was in Williamsburg, Virginia. That evening, he conducted a procedure to insert a bypass until the surgery for the stone removal would take place after New Year's.

Many of you are asking yourself now, what is the big deal? The big deal for me was the diagnosis that came next. After awakening from surgery, the doctor told me that during the procedure, he found what appeared to be a patch of cancer on my bladder. After receiving the results from the biopsy, he went on to say it was "good cancer" because it was the type that had "only" a 50/50 chance of coming back. For the next two years, I would have to get checked every three months to see if the cancer had returned. During the next eighteen months, all the results came back negative. On my last checkup, before pushing the checks to every six months instead of every three, some growths had returned. I remember the doctor saying, "Sorry, man," as he looked through his scope.

I remember only some of what he said after that because I was still processing the possibility of cancer returning. He said something about the cancer no longer being the "good" kind because it had returned. Looking back, I am grateful for the kidney stone. If not for it, I would not have known about the cancer resting on my bladder. The cancer could have penetrated the inner layers of my bladder if left untreated. Often, the symptoms associated with this type of cancer remain dormant until the disease is at a later stage, whereby treatments are more complicated, less effective, and the prognosis direr.

At the beginning of this book, I remarked that everyone has a story to tell. I also forewarned that something was coming your way right now. Your personal and professional crucibles are unplanned, unexpected, and unwanted – but they will come your way just the same. It is never a question of if, only when. Moreover, when they arrive, the next problem is, are you equipped to lead yourself through them to successfully lead yourself and others in both your personal and professional life?

I have connected our adversity to leadership challenges or crucibles throughout this text. Since this is a book about leadership, such comparisons are warranted. However, spirituality's role in our everyday being is an even more important consideration in leading yourself and others. The spiritual dimension of leadership is often given short shrift, if any at all. I believe this is a mistake. Early in this book, I mentioned that none of us accomplishes anything of significance without the help of others. I would not have done anything meaningful without the guidance and strength that God provided me in executing his will. When we surrender ourselves to something bigger than ourselves, we are in awe and gratitude for his grace.

In many ways, my story is the same as yours. You have and will continue to face adversity in your life. Your account includes your professional one as well. It is not what you are but who you are that matters. I can be defined superficially by what type of car I drive, what kind of job title I hold, and what type of degrees I possess.

What is more important is how I am defined by who I am as a friend, son, husband, colleague, and leader. Over the years, I have joked with my wife by saying, "Marian, on my gravestone, I want the inscription 'I did not see that coming,'" referring to the finality of death. And so it is true with my story here. I never saw what was coming my way in advance, and neither will you. We can prepare ourselves by changing things about ourselves to make us better leaders of ourselves and those we lead. Dealing with change is hard. Changing something about ourselves is even more challenging. However, most of us have not tapped into the capacity and resilience already built within all of us to overcome the most trying of circumstances. We miss out when we disregard the power of spirituality and the application of the spiritual dimension of leadership.

While we are not entirely in charge of our lives, we can direct its path. I always tell my young nieces and nephew, "Look at your life as a movie with you being the script's writer." While encouraging them to dream big and open themselves to being receptive to all of life's possibilities, I always end my conversation with them by posing a question: "What type of movie will your life be?" Our lives can also be viewed as a movie, and, as the writers of our script, we can always change the narrative. All of us have or will face what, at the time, will seem to be insurmountable challenges. The good news is that we can alter our course and change the ending. My faith in God provides me with a sense of hope and gives me the courage to continue to walk down my life path.

I hope that this book has many takeaways for you. In finding out who you are, I hope all of you have found a better way to lead yourselves. When life comes your way, the most critical issue is how you will react in leading yourself and others. There is no better time to make the necessary changes and learn to lead as you have never led before. Good luck!

"The trouble is, you think you have time."

– Jack Kornfield

BIBLIOGRAPHY

Adams, Scott, *The Dilbert Principle: A Cubicle's-eye View of Bosses, Meetings, Management Fads, and Other Workplace Afflictions*. New York: HarperCollins Publishers, Inc., 1996.

Aristotle, *The Ethics of Aristotle*, trans. J.A.K. Thomson. Penguin Books, New York, 1976.

A Testament of Hope: The Essential Writing of Martin Luther King, Jr., ed. James Melvin Washington. Harper & Row, San Francisco, 1986.

Bennis, Warren. *Managing People Is Like Herding Cats: Warren Bennis on Leadership*. Provo: Executive Excellence Publishing, 1999.

Bennis, Warren. *On Becoming a Leader*. New York: Perseus Books, 1989.

Bennis, Warren, and Robert Thomas. *Geeks and Geezers: How Era, Values, and Defining Moments Shape Leaders*. Boston: Harvard Business School Press, 2002.

Bennis, Warren, and Patricia Ward Biederman. *Still Surprised: A Memoir of a Life in Leadership*. San Francisco: Jossey-Bass, 2010.

Bennis, Warren, and Joan Goldsmith. *Learning to Lead: A Workbook on Becoming a Leader*. 4th ed. New York: Basic Books, 2010.

Bennis, Warren, and Robert Thomas. *Crucibles of Leadership*. Boston: Harvard Business School Press, 2011.

Covey, Stephen M. R., and Rebecca R. Merrill, *The SPEED of Trust: The One Thing that Changes Everything*. New York: Free Press, 2006.

Covey, Stephen R. *The 7 Habits of Highly Effective People*. New York: Fireside, 1990.

DePree, Max. *Leadership Jazz*, New York: Doubleday, 1992.

Depree, Max. *Leadership Is an Art*. East Lansing, Michigan: University of Michigan Press, 1988.

Drucker, Peter. "Leadership: More Doing Than Dash." *The Wall Street Journal*, 6 January 1988., Dow Jones & Company, Inc.

Duckworth, Angela. *Grit: The Power of Passion and Perseverance*. New York: Scribner, 2016.

Fastabend, David, and Robert Simpson. *Adapt or Die: The Imperative for a Culture of Innovation in the United States Army.* http://www.au.af.mil/au/awc/awcgate/army/culture_of_innovation.pdf

Gardenswartz, Lee, and Anita Rowe, *Diverse Teams at Work.* Burr Ridge, Ill.: Irwin Professional Publishing, 1994.

Gardenswartz, Lee, and Anita Rowe, "The Effective Management of Cultural Diversity." In *Contemporary Leadership and Intercultural Competence: Exploring the Cross-Cultural Dynamics Within Organizations*, Michael A. Moodian, ed. Thousands Oaks, California: SAGE Publications, 2009.

Gardner, Howard. *Leading Minds.* New York: HarperCollins, 1995.

George, Bill. *Authentic Leadership.* San Francisco: Jossey-Bass, 2003.

George, Bill, Peter Sims, Andrew N. McLean, and Diane Mayer. "Discovering Your Authentic Leadership." *Harvard Business Review*, February 2007.

George, Bill, Peter Sims, Andrew W. Malone, Wanda J. Orlikowski, and Peter M. Senge. *Discovering Your Authentic Leadership.* Boston: Harvard Business School Press, 2011.

George, Bill. *Discover Your True North: Becoming an Authentic Leader.* Hoboken, New Jersey: John Wiley & Sons, 2015.

George, Bill. "Truly Authentic Leadership." *US News and World Report*, October 30, 2006.

Gergen, David. *Eyewitness to Power: The Essence of Leadership: Nixon to Clinton*. New York: Touchstone, 2001.

Goffee, Robert, and Gareth Jones. *Why Should Anyone Be Led by You?* Boston: Harvard Business School Press, 2011.

Goldsmith, Marshall. *What Got You Here Won't Get You There*. New York: Hyperion, 2007.

Goleman, Daniel. *Emotional Intelligence: Why It Can Matter More Than IQ*. New York: Bantam Books, 1995.

Goleman, Daniel. *Working with Emotional Intelligence*. New York: Bantam Publishing, 1998.

Goleman, Daniel. *What Makes a Leader?* Boston: Harvard Business School Press, 2011.

Greenleaf, Robert. *Servant Leadership*. Mahwah, N.J.: Paulist Press, 1991.

Greenlief, Robert. "The Servant as Leader." The Greenleaf Center for Servant Leadership, 2008.

Hurley, Robert F., Nicole Gillespie, Donald L. Ferrin, and Graham Dietz. "Designing Trustworthy Organizations." *MIT Sloan Management Review*, June 18, 2013.

Inam, Henna. *Wired for Authenticity: Seven Practices to Inspire, Adapt, & Lead.* Bloomington, IN: iUniverse, 2015.

Kafka, Franz. *Diaries,* ed. Max Brod. New York: Schocken Books, 1949.

Kotter, John. *Leading Change.* Boston: Harvard Business School Press, 1996.

Kouzes, James M., and Barry Z. Posner. *Credibility: How Leaders Gain and Lose It, Why People Demand It.* San Francisco, California: Josey-Bass, 2011.

Kouzes, James M., and Barry Z. Posner. *The Leadership Challenge: How to Make Extraordinary Things Happen in Organizations 5 ed.*) San Francisco, California: Wiley, 2012.

Loden, Marilyn, and Judy B. Rosener, *Workforce America!* Homewood, Ill.: Business One Irwin, 1991.

Luft, J., *Of Human Interaction.* Palo Alto, California: National Press, 1969.

Luft, J. *Group Processes: An Introduction to Group Dynamics* (2 ed.). Palo Alto, California: National Press Books, 1970.

Malandro, Loretta. *Fearless Leadership: How To Overcome Behavioral Blind Spots And Transform Your Organization.* The McGraw-Hill Companies, 2009.

Maxwell, John. *Good Leaders Ask Great Questions: Your Foundation for Successful Leadership.* New York, New York: Hachette Book Group, Inc., 2014.

Nerin, William F. *You Can't Grow Up Till You Go Back Home: A Safe Journey To See Your Parents As Human.* New York: The Crossroad Publishing Company, 1993.

Peters, Thomas, and Robert H. Waterman, Jr. *In Search of Excellence.* New York: Harper & Row, 1982.

Senge, Peter. *The Fifth Discipline.* New York: Doubleday. 1990.

"The Kurt Lewin Change Management Model." www.change-management-coach.com/kurt_lewin.html.

"If you want to lift yourself up, lift up someone else."

– Booker T. Washington

INDEX

For inquiries about speaking engagements, book signings, and training requests, the author can be reached at drclintonmcovert.com